Starfire

KATRINA THOMPSON

ISBN: 1463573057
ISBN-13: 9781463573058
LCCN: 2011909654
CreateSpace, North Charleston, South Carolina

Acknowledgements

There are many people that I would like to thank, but, first and foremost, I would like to thank God for the ability to free my imagination in ways I never thought possible. I would also like to thank my sisters Lakesha McCloud and Ladonia "Pumkin" Hawkins for their love, guidance, and unbelievable support in the pursuit of my dreams. Being the little sister, I've always looked up to you both and your encouraging words have meant so much to me. I would like to thank you Kesha for being there to comfort me when mom and dad couldn't and thank you Pumkin for being my "voice of reason".

To my parents, Leroy and Jessie Thompson, I would like to thank you for your endless support throughout my life. I thank you both for making me smile whenever I was sad and for your direction when I felt lost. For my niece and nephew that endured my moments of clicking away at my computer; thank you for always wanting my attention. The two of you remain my muse. Last but not least, I would like to thank my friends most importantly Tamikia Harvey, who never forgot about me. Even though you moved away and people tried to tear us apart when we were younger, our bond proved to be much stronger. To my friends at work, you know who you are, I thank you for bringing me back to a long forgotten passion of reading.

Thank you for your support!

Katrina

Losing yourself in words is like finding yourself stuck in the pages. But never forget for every blank page you have the opportunity to release your own imagination.

—Katrina Thompson

Contents

Prologue

The crisp air tangled with the fire as it moved its autumn tendrils in the moonlit sky. The tribe members took their seats to listen to Jessie.

"Your dad always knows the best nights to sit out by the fire," Cody leaned over to tell Jacy.

Jacy lifted his finger to tell Cody to be quiet and motioned for him to listen as Jessie began.

"Legend has it that Kaloy, ruler of the universe, was a wise and powerful ruler who could only be seen by those in his realm. No one knows how he came to be, who he was, or if he still exists. But in his realm, he controlled the orbit as if it were mounds of land we humans had fought over years-ago. He delegated to his officer's, named the Latter Kings, control of each of the planets. When it came down to Earth, he ran into a dilemma. Earth had already been in the possession of Yadra. Yadra was a beautiful and powerful temptress with long black hair that curled like snakes upon her head, and blue eyes that were blue like a cloudless sky. Yadra, however, was unable to be ruler, as she was not an officer of the realm. Kaloy decided that since she'd caught the eye of the Sun King, Paytah, the Moon King, Lucero, and the Sky King, Aakesh, he would assign them all equal parts in the Earth's destiny. Whichever won her heart would stand to rule the Earth entirely and reign along with Yadra. Kaloy found humor in each of their quests for her heart, but warned them that they must never use the Earth as their meeting place. They must never defile his creation with their illicit activities. He had coveted each of his planets as a clean and pure sanctity. Only those joined together as King and Queen were allowed to live as such.

"Paytah tried to win her heart, but he found his fight to be futile and bowed out. But Lucero and Aakesh continued fighting for her love. It is unknown how long it took, as time held no meaning to them, but it was Aakesh that came to be victorious. Only they were so immersed in one another that they did not leave Earth. Kaloy learned of their deceit and punished Yadra by having her remain on Earth for all eternity. Aakesh would be forced to watch her from above, never to return to Earth, and he would have to share Earth with both Lucero and Paytah.

"His punishment proved to be unbearable when he learned that she was with child. She gave birth to a son that she named Jerick. Aakesh begged Kaloy to allow Yadra's return, but he was denied. He began to grow bitter as he watched his son grow from afar. Kaloy witnessed his pain and felt sorry for Aakesh, so as a gift he gave Kaloy a way to communicate with his son through his dreams. Still Aakesh grew bitter against his fellow officer's envying Lucero the most, as he had created one of the most beautiful creatures he had ever seen. Her crystal eyes played at the heartstrings of many, and her grace didn't go unnoticed. Jaelyn would dance across the sky, though the other stars hung amongst the evening sky as commanded. Kaloy also took delight in her dancing, naming her Starfire because of her free spirit and the enjoyment that she brought among them. She became the only star that was able to visit Earth. Aakesh saw in Jerick's dreams how his heart danced to the beat of her every movement and that his heart longed to be with her. However, Aakesh knew that it was against Kaloy's wishes. Lucero would never allow Jaelyn to stay on Earth with Jerick, and Kaloy would never allow Jerick to join him. The more Aakesh thought of making his son happy, he realized that if he could get the two of them together, he would have Lucero's most prized possession, and he would grant his son's wishes. He could then force Lucero to give up his control over the Earth. He would possess the majority of the realm so he could then overpower Paytah's clan for his portion for complete control.

"Aakesh told Jerick of his plan to win Jaelyn's heart. For if he did, Aakesh would allow him to command over all the lands, and he would control all that hung amongst the sky.

"Lucero learned of Aakesh's plans and decided that the only way for him to protect his daughter was to defy Kaloy as well. He would descend from the sky and create soldiers, chosen ones created to keep Jaelyn far away from Jerick and to cause him harm if he ever came near. He knew that he could never kill him, but Kaloy never said anything about a few scrapes or bruises.

"Lucero's choice was easy when it came to finding the perfect protectors. He had always been fond of the wolves, Night Howlers as he would call them, for they were loyal and sang his praises into the moonlit sky.

"He was able to speak the language of any creature that walked the Earth and so was able to communicate with his beloved Night Howlers. He went to the leader of the pack and asked that he would allow the sacrifice of the strongest in his pack. With doing so, he would ensure the bond between wolf and mankind, for they would no longer be hunted, but considered a cousin to the men that dwelled in that area.

"The leader accepted his plea with a paw in Lucero's hand and guided him to his ill-fated brother. He thanked the wolf for his sacrifice and ran his blade across the wolf's neck, bleeding him dry. He collected the blood in an urn that he'd brought from his own collection, a pot that we have carried from generation to generation, which is still with us. Lucero then took the blade and ran it across his wrist. Clear blood glistened as it ran down his wrist, into the urn, adding to the blood that was shed by the wolf. He capped it with nearby leaves and walked along the forest until he came upon the Rockne Tribe.

"He walked among their gazes as they all realized that he was a man of power. His robes sparkled like nothing they had seen before. They were woven with rich hues of blue and draped around his hard body like a god. Lucero knew exactly who he needed to speak with, so did not acknowledge them. He walked directly to the chief's hut.

"Chief Long Feather looked at him, knowing that he was a man of purpose. He was a chief in his own right. Flanked behind him were his main hunters, ready to attack, but Chief Long Feather sensed that Lucero came in peace. Lucero could see that he'd chosen the right people and greeted them.

"Lucero explained his misfortune to the chief and his deal with the wolves. He would need for several of their women to carry a child and drink the blood of the wolf. Their sons would have the strength of fifty men and would be able to transform into wolves themselves. Though immortality was not his to give, these men would have the capability to heal themselves.

'Their only duty would be to protect my only daughter, Jaelyn. You will also be handsomely rewarded.' Lucero handed Chief Long Feather a satchel filled with precious jewels. The chief looked at them, but found no need for them. He found the duty bestowed upon his people of greater value. Lucero left the jewels with him anyway, along with the urn of blood. Lucero also asked that one of the children be carried by the wife of the chief so that the chief that ruled over the tribe would ensure that the task be followed.

"The chief's wife, along with four other women, conceived a child and drank the blood as directed. Four of the women and their sons survived, but the fifth woman and her child both perished.

"Kaloy learned of the wolf's slaying and Aakesh's plan, so he summoned them to court. He explained to them how disappointed he was in their actions and saw fit to punish them. His heart felt heavy, as he understood Lucero's actions. Kaloy decided that for his part, Jaelyn would remain on Earth and live her life as a mortal. If Jerick was able to win her heart, Lucero's portion would be given to Aakesh without retaliation. They would then rule the land as Aakesh willed, and Jaelyn's immortality would be restored. However, if Jaelyn denied Jerick, she would be allowed to live as a human and to be loved by a human. Their lives would be short-lived, as the human body would not be able to contain their genetic anomalies. However, before she died, she would produce a female offspring to carry her fate, grow old, and perish.

"Lucero dropped to his knees, as he could no longer bear to hear Kaloy's judgment. Kaloy apologized for his pain, but explained that, though it upset him when he killed the creature for his own needs, it was Lucero's blood being shed that angered him the most, for Lucero belonged to him, and he did not give permission for his blood to be spilled.

"Lucero cried out, as he felt Aakesh was the reason for his disloyalty but he was not being punished.

"Kaloy looked at Aakesh and said, 'My judgment is not over, for his punishment lies on his son's head. Jerick will remain immortal, but he will live his life longing for only Jaelyn. Through her offspring, I will allow her to be reincarnated once each century for the next five hundred years. But if she denies him, and Jerick is unable to win her heart by the last return, the child will perish, and Jerick will continue to roam the Earth alone for all eternity. You, my dear sir, will no longer have any communication with him, and you will continue to watch him suffer for the rest of your days.'"

"Well, did she ever fall for him?" one of the children asked.

"That's a story for another night, young one," answered Jessie with his large grin.

June 25

"Happy birthday!" shouted Elora as she entered Star's room.

Star slowly poked her head from beneath her covers, squinting her eyes from the morning sun. "Is it morning already?"

"Yes, sleepyhead, it's the morning of your birthday, more importantly. Why am I more excited about this than you are?"

"I don't know, Mom, maybe because you're a freak." Star grinned as she lifted herself from her pink clouds of slumber into a sitting position.

"I've had your gift for years, and I couldn't wait until tonight to give it to you." Her mother grinned as she handed Star the long, thin black box. "It's been in the family for years."

Star reached for the velvet box and lifted the lid, revealing a string of silver stars linked together by small metal hoops. There were some stars bigger than the others, but in the center of the bracelet was the largest of them all, which contained a mosaic-like center of stone.

"I love it," said Star as she wrapped her arms around her mother's neck. She pulled the bracelet from the box, placed it around her wrist, and attached the clasp. "I'll never take it off. Thank you, Mom."

"You're welcome, Starfire." Elora looked into her daughter's gray eyes and said, "I'm glad to hear that." She looked down at the bracelet and ran her thumb across her wrist. "This bracelet is a gift in many ways. Always remember that. Okay?"

"Okay," Starfire replied, puzzled at her mother's statement.

"Now, I know it's your birthday, but your studies will still begin at eight thirty."

"Oh, come on, Mom. It's my birthday," countered Star, pouting.

"Oh, all right, nine. Hurry up and take your shower. I'll begin breakfast," Elora said, walking out of Star's bedroom.

Star lay back down and rolled away from the unwanted sunlight. She looked down at her wrist and marveled at the simplistic beauty of her gift.

"Now, young lady!" Elora screamed from the kitchen below.

Star jumped from bed, only grabbing her housecoat on the way to the bathroom. With her hair still wet, she scooped it into a ponytail and rushed as she put on a pair of jeans and a graphic tee that she pulled from her dresser drawer. She could smell the buttermilk pancakes and bacon through the air vents, making her stomach beg for thier entry. She rushed down the stairs and walked into the kitchen.

Her mother placed a cube of butter on the top layer of the pancake mound and said, "Nice of you to join me, birthday girl."

"Well, I had to make my grand entrance," Star replied as she lifted her fork and began to dig in to her mountain of pancakes.

After breakfast, Star thanked her mother and went upstairs for her books. As she collected her schoolwork, she remembered seeing the kids outside catching the bus and wondered if they were ever able to enjoy having a breakfast feast such as she did. Quite often she would watch them running to the bus while a slice of toast hung in their mouth, or a bagel in their hand.

Star had been homeschooled her whole life, unable to make friends like the other children, but she always enjoyed the time that she was able to spend with her mother. But, she put those thoughts away whenever she saw the kids in the neighborhood leaving on dates or piled up in a car as they screamed out the lyrics to their favorite songs. Star had made only one friend during her time in Maryland. Since they moved a lot, Star never got a chance to really make any. She often thought of Kim, who used to live in the house next to them with her older brother and parents, and how she'd had to fill the void after she moved to Florida with her family because of her mother's job.

Star made her way down to the makeshift classroom her mother had created in a side room off from the kitchen. Star could still smell the morning's breakfast looming in the air. The room was equipped with a large chalkboard that her mom had mounted to the wall, a desk placed on the side for her mother, and one for her right in front of the board. Star took her seat and pulled out her paperwork for today's lessons.

School usually lasted for about six hours, but today, Elora ended it early. Elora closed her math book and looked at Star with a curious smirk upon her face.

"What's going on, Mom?"

"Oh, I just thought that you had enough of this for today," she said as she placed her book down on her desk.

"That's a first!" Star sarcastically stated.

"Why don't we do something fun for a change?" Elora rose from her chair and placed her hands on her hips. "It's your birthday, so it's your choice."

"Okay, what happened to my mom?"

"No, seriously. This is part two of your birthday gift. I placed part three on your bed when you were taking your test," Elora said as she pointed toward the door.

"While you're up there, figure out where you would like to go," Elora yelled as Star ran up the stairs.

Star ran to her room and pushed the door open. Her chest heaved in and out as she walked to her bed. Her mom had laid out a periwinkle blue sundress that had little iridescent daisies cascading down the left strap. They then trailed off into ribbons that stopped just after the midriff. Star picked it up revealing a rounded bottom. She measured it against her body and danced with joy. She'd once loved to wear dresses, but had allowed them to hang dormant in her closet. She turned to run back downstairs to tell her mom thank you, but Elora was already at the door.

"I knew you would love it."

"Thanks, Mom," Star replied.

"Have you decided what you want to do?"

It didn't take long for Star to come up with something, but it always made her sad to think about it.

✧ ✧ ✧

Star's father would let her come up to the front seat whenever they waited in the car for her mom. She would pretend that she was driving and asked her dad to teach her how to.

"Sure, once you turn sixteen, we'll go and get your permit," Thomas replied.

"Why not now, Dad?" Star gazed at her dad with her doe-like eyes.

"Because, you can't reach the pedals," laughed Thomas. "Don't worry. I'm sure you'll find many other ways before then to freak your mom and I out."

✧ ✧ ✧

"I want to learn how to drive, Mom."

"Your wish is my command," Elora said, bowing to Star. "You go and get changed, and I'll go and get ready."

Star laid the dress on the bed and took her hair from her ponytail, allowing her curls to fall down her back. She removed her T-shirt and shrugged off her jeans to put on her new dress.

She stood in the front of the mirror, not knowing what to do with her hair.

Elora knocked on the door and slowly opened it. "I figured that's what was taking you so long." Star turned and smiled at her mom. She walked over to her holding two silver pins lined with rhinestones in her hand. "Why don't you ever wear your hair down?" Elora asked as she picked up Star's brush and began to use it on her hair.

"I don't ever know what to do with my hair, Mom," Star replied while shrugging her shoulders.

"I didn't realize how long it had gotten. I guess it's my fault for not helping you keep it up." Elora brushed out the last kinks in Star's hair and told her to turn around. She pulled back strands of hair and placed the pins in to hold it. "There. Look how beautiful you look. Now, how about the next time you don't know what to do with your hair, you wear it down instead of throwing it into one of these?" Elora asked rhetorically holding up Star's ponytail holder. Smiling she reached into her pocket and handed Star the car keys saying, "Now let's get going."

✫ ✫ ✫

Star drove around for almost two hours before they stopped by a diner for dinner.

"That was so much fun. Thanks, Mom."

"No problem, honey." Elora noticed Star's face turn glum. "What's wrong, honey?"

"I, I just wish…"

"You wish your dad was here. Oh, honey, I know it's hard, but you know he's up there watching over you as we speak."

Tears began to well up in Star's eyes.

"Hey, why don't we go to the movies? We can see a comedy or something to cheer you up."

Star shook her head no and wiped her tears away.

"Well then I know what else we can do." Elora smiled and placed money on the table to pay the bill. "Let's get going."

✫ ✫ ✫

"I thought that you said we were going to do something, Mom?" Star yelled out as she locked the door behind herself.

Elora emerged from the kitchen holding something behind her back.

"What's going on, Mom?" Star said with a smile on her face as Elora returned with her short, curly hair flopping in her face and pulled out a bag of chocolate chip morsels. Nothing made Star feel better than chocolate chip cookies.

"Since it's your birthday, I figure we make the ultimate cookie."

"That sounds like a great idea," replied Star.

The two danced around the kitchen to Tchaikovsky's *Nutcracker*. It was always her favorite. Her mom always played instrumentals in house. She felt that music without words allowed its listeners to express their own emotions. Star pulled out two plates and sat down as her mom carved a piece out of the center, just as Star always liked it.

"I just love it when the center is still chewy. You make the best cookies, Mom."

"Only the best for my little girl."

"I'm not so little anymore, Mom. Next year I will be eighteen, and I really want to get away. To travel around the world, you know?"

"About that, honey, you have your whole life to travel. Maybe you should stay local and finish college first."

"Um, I don't know, Mom. I…"

"Well, how about you sleep on it?" Elora replied as she turned away from her, hiding her facial expression about Star's choice.

"Oh, Mom, I'll think about it, okay?"

Elora turned and smiled. "Okay."

Star finished her second slice and headed up to her room. It was still too early for bed, so Star turned on her TV and pulled out her sketch pad to doodle. As Star lay across her bed, her blanket began to nestle her in its lullaby. Hours passed, and Star hadn't realized that she had fallen asleep.

"The pink clouds strike again," Star said to herself as she sat up. Her mom must have come in her room because her comforter was placed around her like a taco shell and her TV was off. Star took off her dress and laid it across her hamper. She traced the flowers with her hand down to the ribbon that fell along the dress. A smirk crawled upon her face as she made a silent vow to herself that she would definitely wear dresses more often.

Star freshened up for bed and prepared herself for slumber when something caught her eye. She looked out the window and noticed that the sky was riddled with stars. She had never seen so many before. At least not that she could remember. Even the moon hung in anticipation, as if it were calling out to her.

She remembered how she used to lay in the grass with her father and gaze at the stars. She loved the feeling of the grass prickling her arms and to hear the animals sing in the night. But what she loved the most was to listen to her father talk about the midnight sky. He used to make up bedtime stories to help her sleep when it got too late. Because he was in the army, he had spent so many of them away from home, but he would say that it was the nights that he spent with her and her mom that meant the most. Starfire felt the same. Unlike most kids, if her father was home, instead of falling asleep with a flashlight dimly lighting the room waiting with her father's voice in the background, she fell asleep under the stars.

Star would never forget the day when her studies were interrupted by the doorbell. She had stayed at her desk, but her mom hadn't returned for quite a while, so she went to see who it was. She remembered seeing a man standing alongside her in uniform and her mother in tears. She'd only seen her mom cry like that when he had gone off to war, so when she saw her face this time, she knew it was because he wasn't returning home.

She hadn't realized that she had started crying until her teardrops fell onto her nightgown, planting wet spots against her skin. She slouched down beneath her sheets and cried herself to sleep.

June 26

"I've seen you before," Star said questioningly as the man with the blue eyes walked over to her slowly.

With a smile on his face, the man responded by saying, "I'm Jerick. I've been watching you for some time now."

"What do you mean?" Star smiled, puzzled at his statement.

Jerick was face-to-face with Starfire now. He brought his hands to her face and looked deep into her eyes. "You're ready."

"Ready for what?"

"I'm yours, and you are mine. We belong to one another. I have waited centuries to touch you, to hold you, to make you my bride, and you are finally ready."

"Your bride?" laughed Star.

"Not just my bride, but my queen. Come to me, Princess Starfire. Come to me, and together we will become one," Jerick pleaded to Star and slowly faded into the distance.

Star became compelled by something beyond her control. It was like all she could see was his piercing blue eyes gazing into hers, pleading for her compliance. Star moved like she was walking on air, and nothing mattered except for Jerick. She had to find him. Something inside of her told her that she had to be with him.

"Star! Star, honey, wake up!" yelled Elora.

Star blinked her eyes uncontrollably, trying to snap herself out of her trance. She felt the air blow up her gown and felt the gravel from the sidewalk prickle beneath her feet.

"Star, honey, are you awake?"

The sight of her mother standing in front of her in her robe confused her.

She blinked her eyes vigorously, trying to understand. She brushed strands of her hair away from her face and asked, "Mom, what's going on?"

"You were sleepwalking."

"Oh…I…I'm sorry, Mom. I don't know what happened," Star said while wiping her face.

"Come on, honey, let's get you back inside." Elora took off her housecoat and threw it over Star as she hung her head in shame.

Star walked up the stairs with her mom, embarrassed about what had just transpired. "I can't believe that just happened," she said as she sat down on her bed.

"Are you okay? You've never walked in your sleep before."

Star lay back and pulled her covers up to her chest. "Yes, Mom, I'm okay. I'm so sorry. I don't know what happened to me. I just want to go back to sleep."

Elora leaned forward and kissed her on the forehead. She looked at Star with her hand still on her cheek. "Are you sure, honey?"

"Yes, I'm sure. Goodnight, Mom," replied Star with a smile on her face.

Star watched while Elora left the room and turned off the light. She rolled over, hugging her pillow and regretting that she had had her mother leave. It felt so real, so unbelievably real. And those eyes, she had seen those eyes before.

What was that?

✳ ✳ ✳

Star put on her undergarments and walked to her closet. "Hum, what should I wear?" she asked herself, staring at the clothes in her closet, tapping her heel on her ankle. She moved top after top to the right of her closet until she came across one of her dresses. It was a magenta sundress her mom had gotten for her last year when she took her out for brunch, but she'd only worn it once.

"Time for a new you, Starfire Ever Moore," she said to herself as she pulled out the dress and put it on. "Now what should I do with my hair?" Star automatically began to brush up her hair and went into her kit to grab her ponytail holder. Then she realized that was the old Star. That's what she would have done two days ago, but this was a new year. She put the ponytail holder back in her hair kit and brushed her hair back down. She brushed the front of her hair over her forehead and pinned the hair back with the pins her mom had given her. She looked in the mirror to see her accomplishment.

"Just one more thing." Star pulled out her lip gloss and applied it with enthusiasm. "I guess that's as good as it's going to get!" She smiled at herself in the mirror and made her way down to the breakfast table.

She felt like she was walking downstairs to meet a prom date, like the girls did on TV. She didn't realize her hand was shaking until she felt her new bracelet slide along her wrist. She grabbed her wrist and looked down at the bracelet that somehow gave her the confidence to continue. She couldn't believe that she was so nervous about her mom seeing that she had put on a dress and did her hair. Then she remembered why she had stopped wearing them. Why she had stopped doing her hair. Why she had stopped caring.

When Thomas would come home after being gone for months, or sometimes over a year, her mom would put her in her prettiest dress to greet him. When she got older, it was she who would pick out her favorite dress and comb out her hair to perfection. Remembering his face when she used to run into his arms made her choke on her tears. She dangled her foot over the next step, not wanting to continue on. She wanted to turn around and change, but instead she took a deep breath and joined her mother in the kitchen.

Her mom almost dropped the eggs on the floor when she saw her. "Starfire, I…" Tears began to well in her eyes.

"Oh, stop it, Mom. It's just a dress," said Star as she sashayed to her seat and waved off her mother's glare.

"Oh, honey, you're beautiful. Not that you weren't beautiful yesterday, but I can't believe you did it without me asking, or helping, for that matter." Elora scooped the eggs out of the pan and sat down at the table with Star. "What made you do all of this?" she asked as she nodded her head.

"I just thought that it was time for a change."

Elora smiled and began to eat.

Star finished her breakfast and came to clear her mother's dishes when she felt Elora's hand on her wrist. "Sit down, honey."

Star sat down with a puzzled look on her face. Elora hardly ever had one-on-one talks with her that seemed that serious. She didn't even look that serious when she had the talk about the birds and the bees, not like Star was ever away from her mother long enough to fly.

"What's up, Mom?"

"I wanted to talk about what made you go outside. Where were you going?"

"Oh, come on, Mom, I don't want to talk about it."

"Please, honey. I need to know," she said, rubbing her hand on Star's.

Star looked at her mom. She knew that look. It had turned from serious to stern. It was the one that she would give whenever Star did something wrong but she wouldn't cop to it. Star could never withstand that look. She blew out a sigh and told her mother about the dream—the intensity in his eyes and the longing she felt for him as she was being pulled back to reality. Her mom was in disbelief.

"Who was he, honey?" Elora said, peering into her daughter's eyes.

"His name?" she responded with a crease in her forehead. "His name was Jerick."

✲ ✲ ✲

Star had never seen her mom's face look like that before. She had a panicked look in her eyes like she had seen a ghost. Her jaw locked in a state of awe. Star didn't know what to do or what else to say.

"Um, Mom? Mom! Snap out of it," Star said repeatedly, snapping her fingers in her mother's face.

"I knew you were the one. I just—It's just so soon."

"I don't understand, Mom. You're babbling."

"Um, no studies for today," said Elora while squeezing out a smile for reassurance. "You can hang out for today. I have some errands to run." She jumped up in urgency and walked swiftly upstairs. She was back downstairs before Star could comprehend what was happening. "Can you clean up the kitchen for me, honey?" Elora asked as she walked out of the door.

Star could've sworn she heard a slight crackling in her mother's voice. She walked to the window and saw her mother wiping her face just before pulling off. Star couldn't understand what had gotten her mother so upset about her dream.

She cleared off the table and began washing the dishes. *What could it have been?* she thought to herself. Nothing that she said could've brought forth such a reaction.

It didn't take Star a long time to finish the dishes, but her mom still hadn't returned. Star didn't know what she could possibly do until her mother returned. She had school Monday through Friday every week, unless her mom chose not to do studies for the day or if it was a holiday, neither of which came around very often.

Star rinsed off her hands and looked down at her uneven nails. "Well, I guess I might as well complete my transformation and do my nails." Before she headed up the stairs, Star looked out the window again for her mom, but all that could be seen were the daisies that swayed along the lawn and the alluring sky that promised a sun-filled day.

Star made her way up to her mom's room and searched through her many shades of red. "Should I be bold and go with fire-engine red or mauve? Maybe fuchsia? No, Paradise Pink!"

Star sat on the floor of her mother's room and groomed her nails. She tried to think of a link between what had happened over breakfast and her dream. She had left so quickly. Fear came upon Star.

Is my mother going to get my psychiatrist because I was sleepwalking and subconsciously walked out of the house to be with some stranger I saw in my dreams? she thought. His words were now imprinted in her mind. *He said that he had been watching me for some time. He wasn't a stranger; I hadn't just met him.*

She waved her hands to dry her nails, put her mother's things back where they had been, and ran to her room.

Elora had taken Thomas's death hard, but Star had stopped eating and barely talked anymore. Because of her catatonic state, Star had fallen behind on her studies and slept most of the day away. Dr. Peterson tried to pull her out of it, but most of their sessions were spent in silence. He had thought that it was probably because she had spent most of her time with her parents that losing one of them may take several months for her to snap out of it. And so it did. Elora was thankful for Dr. Peterson's help, but Star remembered now why she had come back to life. It wasn't her weekly sessions, her grandmother flocking to her side for comfort, or the smell of her mother's abundance of chocolate chip cookies. It was him. She remembered those eyes, that voice. It was Jerick.

Star ran down the hall to her room and pulled out a sketch pad she had drawn in years ago. Pulling back its hard black cover, she thumbed through the pages and found them, the blue eyes. She hadn't written down his name, but scribbled on the edge of the page were three words: *I need you.*

She slammed the book closed and said, "Who is this guy?"

"Would you like some more coffee, darlin'?" the waitress asked Elora.

"Oh, yes, please. Thank you," Elora said with a startled voice. Her mind was a million miles away thinking about what needed to be done.

"Hello, Elora," said a cool voice.

"Hello, Felix," Elora responded, jumped at his presence. He was tall, slender, warm, and smelled like ash, just as she remembered. She noticed the change in the temperature the minute he appeared. His red hair was shorter than she remembered, and was bright against his pale skin, but he still wore his tailored suit and held her attention with his emerald eyes.

He slid down in the seat across from Elora and could see the fear in her eyes. "It will be okay," Felix assured Elora as he reached out his hand and placed it on top of hers. "So she has seen him?"

Elora found comfort in his warm touch. "Yes, last night, in her dreams," Elora replied as she gasped for air. "She was actually trying to go to him. I found her outside in her nightgown and had to shake her awake. I have always known that she was the one, but…"

"She's almost eighteen, Elora. He's aware of her presence and knows that time is running out for the both of them. He knows that this is his last chance."

"What happened with the other four?"

"The first of her kind came without his knowledge and carried out Kaloy's promise to bear a seed that would keep the bloodline going. The second was killed by Jerick's own hand when he found her married with offspring. Jerick did not possess the power that he does now to enter their dreams. That didn't come until after the third of her kind died from the plague at a young age."

"So how do we still exist?"

"Kaloy's promise had to be kept. She wasn't the only child, so her brother kept the bloodline going."

Elora understood and took a sip from her mug.

"The fourth was thought to be crazy because of the dreams that she shared with Jerick and was placed in a mental hospital by her parents. No matter how hard Jerick tried, he could not get to her in time. She had grown too old to withstand the power that awaited her."

"Yes, I remember my mother telling me about her. She said that her mother had her when she was a teenager. She was sent off to be raised by her aunt. But I don't understand. She had fallen for someone else."

"Jerick had not known of her relationship because she was being protected on the reservation. When he found her, she was so lucid that her thoughts and feelings probably weren't conveyed in her dreams. He was able to express his love for her, but his actions became pointless."

"What did you mean by too old for the power?"

"I have to admit, there's parts of the story that have been withheld from you. You do remember the story, right?"

"Yes, I used to tell Star the story all the time when she was little."

"There's a power that awaits Starfire, a power greater than either of us could imagine. But, the power that already lies within her eats away at her every day that goes by. Have you ever noticed her shaking now and again or wondered why you have no living descendants? Your human body can't withstand the power of Lucero. Growing old for you doesn't hold the same meaning for a human as it does to Kaloy. You're here long enough to fulfill his promise of offspring and to raise a child that will carry out Lucero's punishment. Starfire, however, is different. She is the last of her kind, and therefore the power has built up inside of her. If Jerick is unable to fulfill the wishes of his father, Starfire will not need to bear an offspring and therefore not need to continue on as her predecessors did. She will perish on her eighteenth birthday."

Elora's face turned ghostly. "You said that time was running out for both of them. You said that if we kept her hidden, she would be safe. This can't be happening. How could they leave that part out?"

"If you had known, would you have given her to Jerick, sealing the fate of billions, just to save her life, or would you still allow her to choose? Her fate is her choice, but she's protected by me and the Night Howlers to allow her the opportunity to make it. There is still hope for her. She still has a chance to survive this. We have not needed the help of the Night Howlers for some time, but they have been given resources to help keep her alive. They possess a gift from Lucero and Paytah that can prolong her life."

Elora grabbed his hand. "Tell me how."

"Unfortunately I can't tell you, but too much time has gone by. We need to move quickly. Where is the child?"

✵ ✵ ✵

Star always felt weird being home by herself. She was almost an adult, but she was hardly ever left alone. She had never understood why she was always under her parents' watchful eyes. When they lived in Texas, the children there used to make fun of her and call her the Ice Princess, stuck in her castle, staring down with her gray eyes. Her father had found her in the corner of her closet crying about it one day and told her that she was his princess and not to worry about what other kids said.

She had run out of things to do, so she went down to the living room to sketch. She always loved the light that came in from the bay windows. There was a bench that went along the wall, filled with pillows, just the way Star liked it. When her mom was looking for a house there, she had chosen that one because Star loved it so much. She curled up on the bench and let her imagination guide her hand. Only, it was her dreams that were revealed. Jerick's eyes gazed at her from the page below. Star was focused completely on his eyes. Those eyes that had once visited her and brought her comfort now reached into her inner being. Those eyes called out to her. They longed for her, and she couldn't understand why, but she wanted to be with him as well.

I don't even know this man. Star thought to herself. She snapped out of it once she saw her mother's Corolla pull into the driveway. She noticed that there was a silver Audi that followed closely and pulled in behind her. Star put her notebook down so quickly that it dropped to the floor as she went to unlock the door. When she opened the door, her mother was taking things from out of the trunk. Star ran back to the bench and put on her flats. When she got back to the door, she saw her mother behind the car with one hand filled with bags while she pulled what looked like a large duffel bag from the trunk. She then passed the bags over to the tall, slender man who had gotten out of the car behind hers. Together they walked to the door.

"Do you need help with anything else, Mom?" Star asked her mother.

Elora smiled and rolled the bag to Star. "No, sweetie. Here," she said, handing her the bag. "I got you some luggage."

Star took the luggage from her mom, but kept her eyes on the stranger. They all filed into the house and paused in the foyer as Elora locked the door behind them.

"How will I tell her?" Elora whispered to herself.

"Did you say something, Mom?"

"Star, honey, this is Felix. He's a friend of the family."

"You've never mentioned him before," Star responded coyly.

"Star, don't be rude," Elora scolded her.

"I'm sorry, I didn't mean to be rude." She held out her hand and said, "It's nice to meet you sir."

Felix delicately placed the bags in Elora's hand and turned to Star. "It's a pleasure to make your acquaintance, Princess." He reached for her hand and kissed the back of it as if she were a queen.

Star was embarrassed by his greeting and almost shrieked at the warmth of his touch. "Princess." Star cringed. "Um, just call me Star."

"Honey, why don't you take these up to your room and come back downstairs so that we can talk?" Elora said as she took the bags from Felix and handed them to Star. '

Star walked away, still puzzled at their greeting.

Elora motioned for Felix to join her in the living room. "Have a seat. I apologize for her demeanor towards you. She obviously doesn't remember you, and she only allowed her father to call her Princess. Please don't take any offense to her response."

Felix walked into the living room, noticing Star's disheveled notebook lying on the floor. He reached down and gazed at its contents. "Her artistry is so vivid. She draws as if they were sitting for a portrait," Felix marveled.

"She's always been good at that. Whatever you couldn't get her to say, she could draw it for you. I would put that down before she came back, though. She doesn't like for people to look at her sketches without her permission. It's like a visual diary," Elora stated as she sat back on the couch. Felix closed the book and placed it on the bench. He walked over and took a seat across from Elora.

Star rummaged through the bags before she made her way downstairs. In anticipation of finding out what was behind the new luggage and toiletries her mother had purchased, she rushed back downstairs, almost tripping over her feet. If they were going out of town, where were they going? And what did this have to do with Felix?

"Come have a seat next to me, Starfire." Star walked over and obediently sat next to her mother as instructed. Elora pulled her hand to her lap, turning to her, and said, "There's something we have been keeping from you."

"We?" Star replied, puzzled, as she looked at Felix and then back to her mom.

"I'm going about this the wrong way," Elora sighed and brought her hands to her eyes, pulling back strands of hair to put them behind her ears. "Ever since you were placed in my arms, I've known you were the one. I looked into your eyes, and I knew that the stories my mother told me were true, Jaelyn incarnate. My mother, your grandmother, lifted you from my arms and gazed into your eyes. She said, 'Notice how bright they are, like a full moon on a starless night.' She lifted you up into the air and called out, 'Starfire.' We were just going to name you Ever Moore, but we saw the look in Grandma's eyes and couldn't say no," Elora said with a smile. "Do you remember the story about Jaelyn?"

"Yes, I remember some of it," Starfire responded.

Felix leaned forward and said, "Maybe we should help jog your memory." He began the story as Star remembered, but as the punishment of Aakesh and Yadra was mentioned, Star's eyes beamed at the realization of what was taking place.

"Jerick," Star screeched out and covered her mouth.

"So you remember?" Felix asked as he pulled her hand down to her lap.

Star nodded.

Elora pulled back Star's hair for her to look at her. "It's true. It's all true. You are the last of your kind. Jaelyn's light on this Earth ends with you."

"Her light may end, but yours can begin. It's all up to you, Star. Jaelyn perished centuries ago. But you, my dear, can live beyond her years. You and your family may have had to endure her fate, but the outcome is yours. The Night Howlers await your arrival, and there is but little time before Jerick figures out where you are. Your mother tells me that he has already entered your dreams, so we're running out of time. Sooner or later, you will dream of something that will reveal your location."

"Star, honey, do you understand what we're saying to you? Star!"

Star sat there, dazed and confused. This whole time she had been sheltered and locked up so that Jerick couldn't find her. Moving from state to state wasn't just because of her father being in the army. Having no friends, no freedom, and no life was all because of some destiny that five minutes ago she considered a sad fairy tale.

Star shook her head. "No, this can't be true! I don't believe it." Tears welled up in her eyes as she jumped out of her seat with her hands clenched into fists at her side.

"Star, honey, please listen to us. We didn't mean for it to happen this way. We were so close, and I thought that with only one more year to go, everything was going to be okay. I wish your father was here. He always knew how to talk to you."

"Dad knew?" Star stated in a solemn voice.

"Yes, I had to tell him. He knew that he might not be here to watch you grow, but you could just look into the sky and know that someone was always there to comfort you. They're your family."

"My family." Star began to tremble as she ran out of the living room and up the stairs, wiping her eyes along the way.

"Excuse me for a moment," Elora said to Felix as she headed up the stairs behind her. She found Star huddled on the bed, crying on her pillow.

At the sound of her mother's presence, Star turned to her with tears streaming down her face. "Why me, Mom? I don't understand. Why me?"

Elora sat down on the bed and wiped away Star's tears as she hugged her in her arms. "I can't answer that for you, honey, but I do know this: Everyone has their own destiny to fulfill. My destiny was to be a wife to your father, to give birth to you, and to protect you until it was time for you to make your own destiny."

"And what's my destiny?"

"Oh, honey, I can't answer that either. This is your book to write." She released her daughter and took her face into both of her hands and said, "Only the author knows what's to be written."

Elora embraced her daughter again to hide her tears that had begun to pour as well. Her arms fell from Star, and she walked out to the room. "Make sure you pack some winter clothes as well," Elora managed to get out before she left the door way.

Star had never packed for a trip before, unless you considered moving a trip. She stayed at her grandmother's house for a week after her father passed away, but her grandmother had packed for her. Now she had to pack one bag that would contain clothes that would have to last her several months.

Star rolled off of her bed and made her way to the duffel bag that lay in the middle of her bedroom. *Mom must have known that I wasn't going to be happy about this because she hadn't picked just any old piece of luggage, but one with stars laced around it.* Star thought to herself. She opened the bag and found two smaller bags inside. She wiped away the last of her tears and began to pack, carefully stacking in undergarments, tops, bottoms, pj's, sweaters, jackets, a couple pairs of shoes, and the neglected dresses she had vowed to include in her wardrobe. She packed up all of the toiletries her mom had purchased, and hair supplies, into the smallest bag, which had one big star on it. In the medium-sized bag that had *Superstar* written along it, she packed books and some art supplies. She turned around to see if there was something that she was forgetting and saw the picture of her with her parents on the nightstand. She ran over and hugged it to her chest before walking out of the room and closing the door behind her, carrying one bag on her shoulder and dragging the other two behind her. When she reached the bottom of the stairs, she placed the smaller bag and the photo into the larger bag and scoped the room for her mother's.

Elora entered the foyer, along with Felix, carrying a brown leather messenger bag with the initials of *SEM* engraved in a plate on the front of it.

"Mom, where are your bags?" Star questioned with a quiver in her voice, already knowing the answer.

"I'm not going, honey. This is your journey, and it's best if we go our separate ways for now," Elora managed to answer as she held back tears. "I knew this day would come. I just didn't know it would be so hard and so soon. I placed your favorite songs on an MP3 player, and your important papers are in here, like your birth certificate, passport, that kind of stuff," Elora said with a trembling voice.

"Mom." Star began to cry.

"There's other stuff in there that you can check out later." Elora handed the bag to Star and grabbed her daughter for one last embrace. "I know that you will do the right thing. That you will make the right choice." Elora pulled away and held her crying daughter's face in her hands. "Remember that Mommy loves you and we will be together again."

Star's voice was almost gone at this point, but she was able to get out, "I love you too, Mom."

Neither had noticed that Felix had already placed Star's bags into his trunk, until he returned and said, "It's best if we leave now."

Star's limp body had to be dragged to the car as she still clung to the bag her mom had placed there just minutes before. Her attempts to stop crying were futile. Felix was uncertain how to calm her, so he reached over and tapped her hand. "You're not going to make this road trip any fun if you cry the whole way there."

Star's eyes flickered at his comment. He had seemed so composed at the house, almost like a statue, and now he was joking with her.

He glanced over to Star with his crescent-shaped eyes and smiled. "It's not every day a girl finds out she's a princess, you know."

"You forgot all about the immortal beloved that wants to take over the world," she responded as she wiped away her tears.

"There you go. That's the pretty face I remember."

"I remember the story now. You were never mentioned." It was Star that now glanced at Felix.

"My story didn't begin like that of Jerick and Jaelyn. I was created as another form of protection for you Pri...ah, Star. I am a tracker, an officer of Paytah, an extension of his power here on Earth."

Star was amazed and still curious. "Tell me more."

"After your great-grandmother was tormented by Jerick, Kaloy thought it would be best to have the last of your kind, you, remain with her parents, but still isolated, and only I would know of your whereabouts. I checked in on you and kept in touch with your mother, not to intervene until I was needed. The wolves would only be used if Jerick contacted you."

Star sat silent as the seriousness of the situation hit home. This whole time she had been kept away to protect her and to protect the world from Jerick.

Felix could see by Star's lack of response that she was finally on the same page.

✬ ✬ ✬

Hours passed by in silence, until Felix turned to Star and said, "How about we get you something to eat?" He pulled over to Cracker Barrel and got out of the car. He made his way over to Star's door before she could get out. "After you." He gestured for Star to exit the vehicle. They walked into the restaurant with eyes gazing upon them.

"We must really look odd together," she giggled.

"Not as weird as that couple." He pointed to a guy who was shorter than what appeared to be his wife by at least two feet. She hid her laughter from the other customers and stepped behind one of the doll displays.

They were seated fairly quickly near a back window, as Felix requested. "Away from curious eyes," he whispered and nudged Star as they slid into their seats.

Shortly thereafter the waitress walked over and said, "Hi, my name is Wonda. I'll be your waitress today. Can I start you all with something to drink?"

"I'll just have some water, please?" Star replied.

"Nothing for me. Thank you," Felix said, waving his hand.

"You're not going to eat anything?" asked Star.

"I don't need to eat. When you're immortal, nothing kills you. Not even hunger."

Star leaned in and asked, "How old are you anyway?"

"Oh, a little over two hundred years old. I don't really keep count anymore. After a while you begin not to care."

"So where do you live?"

"I…"

Just then the waitress returned with Star's water. "Here you go. Are you ready to order?"

"I'll just have a cheeseburger and fries."

She wrote down Star's order and asked Felix, "You're sure I can't get you anything?"

Felix smiled and waved. "No, thank you, ma'am."

She picked up the menus and threw Felix a suspicious look as she walked away.

"So…?"

"So what?" Felix replied.

"So where do you live?"

Felix gave her a slight grin and crossed his hands on the table, saying, "Wherever you live."

"Texas?"

"Lived."

"South Carolina?"

"Lived."

"Maryland?"

"Lived."

"So how can you afford to move as we do?"

"Let's just say I have direct access to some of the Earth's greatest treasures."

Star looked at him, puzzled at his statement.

"Humans have to wait thousands of years in order to possess some of the most precious stones, but I can go get them myself." He smiled and tapped his pinkie finger, which was garnished with an emerald stone encased in a gold setting, on the table. "I was created by Paytah, remember? The power of the sun is in me. It's also your source of survival."

"Here you go, sweetie." The waitress placed the plate of food in front of Star. "Enjoy."

"Thank you," replied Star. "So what were you saying?"

"Your mother doesn't work, Star. How did you think she could afford all that you had?"

"I never really thought about it before." She shrugged.

"Well, several of the jewels were sold, and the money was placed into a deposit box, savings account, and stocks. Your family has lived off of it for decades. They only use what they need to live comfortably and discreetly."

"So I'm secretly rich?"

"You are a princess, after all."

Star pursed her lips, eyeing her sandwich.

"I'm sorry. I forgot you don't like to be called that."

Star ate her meal as quickly as she could while Felix looked from the window to the wandering eyes in the restaurant. Star found it all amusing, but she could tell that Felix grew tired of their constant glares.

"Where are we headed?" Star asked as she finished her meal.

"If I tell you, you'll tell Jerick, and all of this would've been for nothing."

"No, I wouldn't."

"Not consciously, but subconsciously."

Star understood, but still questioned it, as she had known where she lived before and had dreamed of Jerick.

Felix didn't utter another word on the matter. He gazed out the window and said, "You better use the bathroom before we go."

Star nodded, scooted out of her seat, and headed to the restroom just as the waitress stopped by with the check and collected the dishes.

"Can you bring another glass of water?" Felix asked Wonda.

"I sure can." She returned to the table with his request before Star came back.

"Thank you." Felix smiled and handed her a fifty-dollar bill. Her eyes widened as the corners of her mouth met them with glee, and she scurried away. Felix pulled the glass over to him, lifted the face of his ring to pour out its contents, and pushed it back to the other side of the table as Star rejoined him. "You better drink up because I don't plan on stopping for a while."

Star obediently replied by drinking down almost every drop.

The treetops painted a border against the evening sky as the sun began to take its rest. Star started to feel sleepy, so she had to make conversation. "Okay, I get that you don't want me to know where we're going, but how are you going to keep me from knowing when we get there?"

"Oh, I have my ways, and the Night Howlers have theirs." Felix beamed.

"Well, what are your ways?" Star yawned and adjusted herself in her seat as she tried to resist the slumber that awaited her.

"It appears that you'll soon find out."

Only Starfire never heard the end of his statement. She succumbed to the sleeping powder that Felix had emptied into her drink as Felix smiled and drove into the night.

June 27

He pulled into the Long Feathers' driveway just before dawn while Star still lay in the passenger seat of the car, lightly snoring. Felix gently moved strands of hair away from her face and stroked her cheek as Jessie and Jacy walked over to the car. Felix stepped out and unlocked the truck.

"Good morning, Felix," said Jessie as he walked over and shook his hand. "Jacy, can you come and get her bags?"

Felix opened the trunk door and handed the bags over to him. Jacy took her bags inside as Jessie and Felix talked. "Here's enough to cover anything she might need during her stay," Felix stated and handed Jessie a yellow envelope stuffed with money.

"You don't have to worry. We'll take good care of her."

Felix bit his lip, holding back the thoughts that clouded his mind. "I know that you will." He made his way over to the passenger door and opened it as Jacy returned. "She's still asleep. She might wake up a little groggy, and she'll most likely be upset with me for leaving her with strangers." Felix laughed as he scratched his head.

Jessie walked over, saying, "Ah, I've had to deal with a teenage girl before. Between Ruth and I, we can handle it."

Jacy bent down and looked inside. He reached over to unbuckle the seat belt and looked at Star. His eyes froze upon her face. He had never seen anyone so beautiful before. She was her former self, but there was something different about her.

"Is there something wrong, son?" Jessie questioned Jacy as he peered over Felix's shoulder.

"Ah, no, Dad," Jacy replied as his cheeks burned in embarrassment. He tried to compose himself and lifted Star's arm around his shoulder, grabbed her flats, and lifted her from her seat. *She smelled of lavender in a summer breeze,* Jacy thought to himself as he carried her inside.

Jessie looked over at Felix and could see his worrisome glare. He placed his hand on his shoulder and with his warm smile said, "Don't worry. She'll be safe with us."

Felix nodded to Jessie, hopped into his car, and drove off.

✭ ✭ ✭

Star awoke groggy and confused, just as Felix had predicted. *Where am I?* she thought to herself as she fought to open her eyes. They rolled beneath her eyelids and blinked open to the afternoon sun that poked through, begging her to join the day while her hands searched for something recognizable, but all she found were blankets.

Wasn't I in the car with Felix? Maybe this is all a bad dream. It can't be. Though the bed was comfortable, she knew it wasn't hers. She lifted her head and began to look around, still a little woozy, but she had to figure out where she was. She peered around the pale walls of the room, but she didn't recognize anything. There were no photos or decorations adorning them. She saw a desk that was pushed against it on her left and on the right there was a dresser with a small lamp on top. There was a door next to it, probably a closet, Star thought. She pulled back the covers and swung her legs out of the bed. Her shoes were waiting in line on the floor beneath her feet. She slid them in and noticed her bags on the floor at the bottom of her bed.

"Night Howlers," Star whispered. *Felix must have drugged me and left me with them.* "I'm going to kill him," Star whispered angrily.

She stood up, holding on to the bed for a moment to steady herself, and then she walked over to what she presumed to be the closet door and opened it. Inside she found it to be empty aside from a hanging organizer and hangers. Star ran her hand through her hair and went over to the dresser. There she found several tops, sweaters, and jeans folded meticulously. Star blushed through her caramel-colored skin when she came across the drawer that contained tank tops and boxer shorts. She closed it so quickly it made a loud noise. Star stood still, hoping that no one had heard her intrusion.

Suddenly, she heard footsteps coming closer and closer. Star quickly flipped off her shoes and hopped back into bed.

A woman appeared at the door. She lightly tapped on the door and walked in. Her cheekbones were high, just like her grandmother's, with a slight hint of pink. They rose upon her face when she said, "Hello, honey. We thought that you would never wake up." She walked over to the bed. "My name is Ruth, Ruth Long Feather. It's nice to finally meet you." Ruth smiled. "Why don't you get freshened up so that you can meet the family? The bathroom is the first door on the right. There are fresh towels in the cabinet. When you're done, you can meet us downstairs, and I'll make you some lunch. How does that sound?"

"Okay," Star replied.

Ruth smiled and walked to the door.

"Thank you," an embarrassed Star blurted out before she was gone. She fell back on the bed and giggled to herself.

☆ ☆ ☆

Star walked down the stairs shaking just as she had when she'd dressed up the day before. She didn't have the courage to wear a dress today, so she'd put on a frilly tank top and jeans to meet her new guardians. In her hair, she wore the pins her mom had given her on her birthday. Wearing them made her feel a little bit closer to her.

The stairs led right down into the kitchen/dining room area. To her left she saw Ruth placing her lunch on the kitchen table. Her warm spirit reminded her so much of her mom. She wore her hair in a single fishtail braid down her back, and a knitted sweater with wolves dotted along the bottom. A good idea, Star thought, as the morning chill still dangled in the air. She could hear people talking through the doorway that led to the family room. Star felt eyes gazing upon her as she walked closer to the doorway, but she was too nervous to meet them.

"What happened to Felix?" Star asked Ruth as she walked over to the table.

Ruth walked over to the table with a serene smile and said, "Felix's duties are over for the time being. It's our turn to care for you now. Here, have a seat." Ruth pulled out the chair in front of the sandwich and patted it.

Star sat in the chair and dove into her meal.

"Everyone wants to meet you, but you take as much time as you need to eat. We'll be waiting in the living room when you're done," Ruth stated as she walked out of the room.

Star took her advice and took twice as long as it normally would to eat. She was always so scared to meet new people. She remembered when she met Kim and her brother Clark for the first time. It was a little easier with them. They'd hit it right off, but when she met Kim's parents, she hardly ever spoke in their presence and used Kim to speak for her if she needed to ask them something. She didn't get used to them until a year later, but by that time, it was time for Kim and her family to move away.

She had to face it. This is the place she was going to have to live in for the next couple of months, whether she liked it or not, so she better get used to it. Star finished her meal and discarded the foam plate in the trash. She straightened her top and slowly made her way to the living room door.

"Come on in," Ruth called out to Star.

Star walked into the living room and was suddenly taken aback by the heat wave that encamped about the room.

Ruth, still wearing her knitted sweater, noticed Star's face flush as she walked over. "Sorry, honey, the heat is something you have to get used to when you're living with wolves. They run at a hundred-ten degrees, and when you have three of them in a room, it can be a little overwhelming." Ruth smiled and pulled her over to a man sitting on the sofa, passing by two guys who sat in chairs by the fireplace, and a girl holding a sleeping child.

Star glanced over at the fireplace with a slight grin. She thought they probably never had a need for a fireplace. Star felt so nervous that her legs felt wobbly beneath her.

The tall, husky man stood up and with a deep voice said, "My name is Jessie Long Feather. Welcome to our home."

Star smiled as she noticed how youthful the man looked compared to his wife. But she could tell he was much older by the wisdom behind his eyes. *You can always tell by the eyes,* Star thought to herself. "Thank you, sir."

"You've already met my wife, Ruth." He stretched out his arm to the girl sitting on the wraparound couch. "This is our eldest daughter, Kaya, and her daughter Chenoa."

"Nice to meet you, Princess." She smiled.

Star pulled her hair behind her ear. With an awkward smile, she replied, "Oh, just call me Star."

Ruth went and sat down as Jessie grabbed Star's hand and took her over to meet the others in the room. "This here is Stephen Monroe and my son Jacy," Jessie stated as he kicked Stephen's chair to stand up.

"Sorry, Prin—ah, Star. It's nice to meet you," Stephen managed to get out beyond his side grin to Jacy.

She looked over to him as well and found that Jacy's face was hard and difficult for her to read as he stood up and stepped over to her. She felt her heart skip, possibly out of the fear of his cold, dark eyes that peered down at her, or at his deep, husky voice.

"Nice to meet you," he said without a change in his demeanor.

"The two of them, myself, and two others make up the 'still active' pack," Jessie said while making air quotes with his hands. The others have retired from the Night Howler business, but are always connected. You'll meet Cody and Poe later. Oh, and of course, let's not forget Grandpa Joe. He still chimes in when he wants, but I haven't seen him shift in years. Now come over and have a seat. We need to talk."

Star walked back over to the other side of the room and took the corner seat of the couch as Jessie returned to his seat.

"I'm guessing by now you realize how important this is."

Star nodded yes.

"You'll be with us for at least a year, so your safety and well-being is our main concern."

At least a year, Star thought to herself. Neither her mother nor Felix had told her it would be at least a year.

"With that being said, we have a couple of rules that you'll need to follow in order to ensure that that's what takes place." Jessie looked directly at Star. Her stomach lurched in fear as she wrapped her arms around it to console it.

"Jacy will be your main protector. You will be staying in his room for the duration of your stay. He will be sleeping on the couch and will only enter the room for clothing or to check on you."

"I don't want to be an inconvenience. I can sleep on the couch. I don't mind," Star blurted out.

"No, the decision has already been made. This is what's best. The other rule is that you're not allowed to watch TV unless it's a movie or taped program that doesn't reveal our whereabouts."

Star gazed at the flat screen that was mounted on the wall and all of the unopened DVDs that lined the shelves below.

Jessie noticed the movement in her eyes and smiled. "I've recently had Jacy stock our video collection with things you may like to watch. There's one more rule. If you decided to go outside, you are limited to the forest behind the house and down the street. Only Grandpa Joe and Poe's family lives on this street. We acquired this area a while back, so the forest always has one or two of us lurking around. You'll always be protected. Remember, your location needs to be kept as a secret not only to you, but to Jerick as well."

Star understood why Jessie had made those rules, but it didn't make the situation any better. She had left her jail cell at home only to move into a high-security prison wherever she was.

Kaya must have seen Star's reaction swimming across her face, so she handed her daughter, who had begun to wake up, over to her mother. She turned to Star and said, "Hey, why don't we go upstairs and unpack your clothes? You know, get you settled in." She grabbed Star's hand and pulled her from the couch. Star didn't snap out of it until the cold air of the kitchen hit her like a ton of bricks as they walked upstairs.

They entered the room that Star now shared with a boy she'd just met. She stood silent. Her mind was circling around the notion that this was now her cell and that her fellow inmate had more privileges than she did.

"Oh, come on, it's not that bad. Well..."—Kaya made a face—"it kind of is, but think of it this way: your sacrifice is saving the world."

"Yeah, just call me inmate number seven-seven-seven."

"See? That's the spirit!" Kaya picked up the unopened brown messenger bag Star's mother had given to her.

"Ah, no, not that one," Star screeched out and took the bag from Kaya.

Kaya began to hang up Star's dresses while she folded her tops and placed them in the hanging compartments.

"So you live here too?" asked Star.

"Yeah, it felt like a prison to me too not so long ago," she laughed. "I found out the hard way that if I would've just followed the rules given to me, I wouldn't have been divorced and taking care of a baby on my own. Thankfully my parents took me back in, but unfortunately for you, I took your room."

"My room?" Star asked.

"Technically it was made up for you years ago, after I had left the house. They thought that the room down the hall was too small for you, so they made it up for Chenoa. Jacy and I played the old rock, paper, scissors game to see who would give up their room when we knew for sure you were coming."

"Wait, you knew years ago?"

"Yeah, you didn't?" Kaya pointed and placed her hand on her hip.

"No, I just found out yesterday morning," Star replied as she slid down the wall behind her.

Kaya sat next to her and said, "Don't be upset. I'm pretty sure it was for your own good. Believe it or not, I remember when Felix came and told us. I was only five, and Jacy was just a baby. I don't remember everything that was said, but I do remember those green eyes, pale skin, and his long red hair. Does he still look the same?"

"Still pale, but his hair is probably shorter than you remember," Star replied and laughed.

"So Jacy's known this whole time as well?"

"Oh yeah. He's Dad's prodigy. The kid has been mind-warped into devoting his life to you. No offense, of course."

Star's eyes popped open in surprise.

"I don't think you've fully grasped the importance of being the chief of guards to protect the last Starfire." Kaya saluted. "My father knew that this would be the last opportunity for us to prove ourselves as the guardians of Jaelyn incarnate after the last debacle and to protect the most important one of them all. Jacy was conditioned to be the strongest out of the pack. He got straight As in school, and technically he is the smartest out of the whole bunch. I remember growing up and watching them as they practiced fighting techniques, or my father having council meetings with them and their parents on their progress. You may feel like you're in a jail, but just imagine how they may have felt, growing up knowing that they were going to be responsible for protecting the world's last hope at the age of nineteen."

"That must be why Jacy hates me." Star pouted.

"What are you talking about, Star? He doesn't hate you. He's just trying to figure you out. He's like that with everyone until he gets to know you." Kaya stood back up and reached for Star. "Let's finish up so that we can go and help Mom get dinner started. You have to get started early when you're cooking for a couple of overgrown animals."

Star smiled and joined Kaya. "You mentioned something about some other debacle?" she questioned her.

"Another story for another day." Kaya turned and shouted, "Tada! All finished."

Just then a humming noise buzzed from the bag on Jacy's former bed. "Sounds like you have a phone call." Kaya motioned with her finger and skated out of the room. "I'll meet you downstairs."

Star had never had a cell phone, but she'd never looked in the bag to see what her mom had packed. She walked over to the bed and opened the bag, searching for the phone. Beneath folders and a tinier bag she saw the bright light of the phone. Her mom must have put one in there to keep contact.

"Hello, baby, is that you?"

"Mom," Star replied as tears welled up in her eyes.

"Oh, honey, how are you? Are you safe?" she asked frantically.

"Yes. I don't know where I am, but everyone seems nice. I mean, I just met them."

"Oh, I'm happy to hear that. Is Felix there with you?"

"No, he left already." Star left out the whole drugging incident, knowing that her mother would flip out.

"Did you get to look at the stuff I put in your bag?"

"Not yet, Mom."

"Well, when you do, call me if you have any questions. I'll keep my phone on me at all times. Okay?"

"Yes, Mom."

"I love you, Starfire."

"I love you too, Mom." Star stared at the phone and slunk on the bed. She put the phone down and reached into the bag to reveal its contents. Star found a plastic folder filled with what looked like important papers, the MP3 player, and a small leather envelope. She unsnapped the button and opened it. A stack of money lay inside with a paper band around it that said: *$10,000.* Star couldn't believe it. She hardly ever dealt with cash when she was with her mom. She never even asked for money. Her mom and dad paid for everything. The only time she paid was when the ice cream truck would come around or her mother gave her money to shop for Christmas presents. Now her mom had given her control over thousands.

Star shoved the money back into the envelope and reached into the bag to see what else was left. She found a book lying in the bottom of the bag. She pulled it out and realized it was a photo album. It was more than that. It was a collage of her life. The front of it showed a picture of her as a newborn and read *Starfire* in silver letters. She opened it slowly, going page after page showing different stages of her life with her parents and grandparents. Star couldn't finish it. She hugged the book and lay on the bed crying.

✡ ✡ ✡

Star hadn't realized how much time had gone by until the room had turned dim. She sat up and went to the bathroom to freshen her face before she headed downstairs.

"We thought that we were going to have to call the pack to come and get you. What took you so long?" Kaya said to her sarcastically.

"Oh, stop prying, Kaya. Let the girl have a moment to herself." Ruth shot a smile at Star and continued cooking.

"Well, I'm here now. How can I help?"

"Here, stir this," Kaya replied as she handed Star a spoon.

Just then Chenoa peeped around the corner with her teddy bear in one hand and a sippy cup in the other. She came over to Star and pointed her sippy cup at her, asking, "Who are you?"

Star turned and smiled. "My name is Star. You must be Chenoa."

"How did you know?" she asked with her squeaky little voice.

"Your grandfather told me." Star smiled and bent down to the little girl. "Who's that?" she asked, pointing to Chenoa's bear.

"This is Bear," Chenoa replied and returned to the living room.

"Wow," Kaya stated, amazed at Chenoa's response.

"What?" Star asked.

"She never talks to people she doesn't know. She gets that from her uncle. She must really like you," she replied and took dishes from the cabinet. "Why don't you help me set the table?"

Star put the spoon down on the counter to help. Kaya passed Star the silverware, and she folded the napkins. "What are you smiling about?"

"Oh," Star replied, "I didn't realize that I was. It just reminded me of setting the table with my mom."

Kaya grinned and said, "Help me with the glasses."

She handed her the last glass, and Star's hand began to shake. As if in slow motion, Star saw the glass slipping out of her hands. Suddenly, out of nowhere, a hand reached out and caught the glass before it hit the ground. Jacy looked up at Star and smiled.

"I'm so sorry." Star stumbled backward and steadied herself with the back of a chair.

"Look, no harm, no foul. It didn't even touch the floor." Jacy stood up and placed the glass on the table.

"Is that Grandpa Joe I hear?" Kaya asked.

"Yeah, Dad thought he should meet our new houseguest." Jacy pointed his thumb over at Star.

Just then Grandpa Joe appeared around the corner and shouted, "Something smells good!" He was an older jolly man with silver hair that lay upon his shoulders, and his eyes were dark yet friendly. Not quite like Jacy's, which still scared Star.

"So this must be Starfire." He walked over and wrapped his big, warm arms around her for a bear hug. "We've been waiting for you for some time now. Where have you been hiding?"

Star laughed, "Maryland mostly, I guess."

"Well, we're glad to have you here with us now."

"Yeah, wherever here is."

Grandpa Joe put her down and made his way to the table. "Well, it's best for all of us if you don't know."

The rest of the gang filed into the kitchen.

"Princess," Jacy called out to Star and motioned for her to come over.

Star gave him an evil glance, but filtered through the crowd and went over to see what he wanted.

"This is my cousin, Poe Long Feather, and this is Cody Lightwood."

"Hey welcome to…Just joking. It doesn't matter where you are now that you're with family," Cody laughed.

Jacy nodded at Cody, who immediately wiped the smile off of his face and headed over to the table.

"What was he talking about?" Star asked Jacy.

"Nothing. Let's eat."

✫ ✫ ✫

After dinner everyone went into the family room while Jacy stayed to clean up the kitchen. Star saw that he had stayed behind and figured that helping him just may break the ice between the two of them.

"I'll help you," Star offered and handed him one of the plates off of the table.

"No, thanks. I can handle it myself. Besides, you don't have such a good track record with dishes," Jacy replied.

A crease formed in Star's brow. She pulled out one of the chairs and sat down. "Then I'll just sit here and watch." Star shocked herself with the choice of her words. She was never that bold before, but she figured she had to open up sooner or later. She figured she was already on a roll, so why stop now? "So why are you avoiding me? I mean, if we're supposed to deal with each other for a year, we should really get to know each other. Or do you really hate me that much?"

Jacy smiled. "I don't hate you."

"Great, now that we have that out of the way, why are you avoiding me?"

"I'm not. I just…um. How about you hand me those glasses over there?"

Star smiled, retrieving the glasses and the rest of the dishes from the table, while he took care of the ones that were already on the countertop. They finished cleaning up the kitchen and headed into the family room to watch TV with the others. They stayed up late that night watching classic eighties films and feasting on popcorn and soda. Star was having fun, but grew tired. She didn't want to be rude, so she fought off her sleepiness with a little caffeine.

A couple of hours later, one by one they headed home and off to bed, until only Jacy, Poe, Cody, and Star remained behind. Star stayed up even though Kaya had gone to bed. She found their company quite enjoyable. She had never experienced anything like that before. They were like one big happy family. Cody was the youngest one in the room, always ragged on and used to fetch a drink or whatever anyone wanted. He was the jokester, with Poe not too far from taking the title himself. Jessie and Ruth were the parental units who still kept everyone in check and enjoyed displaying their love. Star saw them several times throughout the night cuddling or stealing kisses from one another. Grandpa Joe kept Chenoa entertained whenever she broke away from questioning Star. Stephen was quiet and composed. And of course, Jacy took it all in and made sure the movies kept going.

Still the night called her. She wished them all a good night and headed upstairs.

Jacy called her as she walked upstairs. "I better get some clothes before you head off to bed." He pulled out a couple of things, including some undergarments, which made Star blush. "Oh by the way, if you ever want to see my drawers, all you have to do is ask," Jacy said with a smile on his face.

Star covered her face with her hand to cover her laughter and embarrassment. "I'm so sorry. I was just trying to figure out where I was." She walked over to him and whispered, "How did you know?"

"I heard you," Jacy replied as he pointed to his ear. "And by the way, as much as you may want to kill Felix for dumping you here, I'm glad that he did." Jacy turned to Star and said, "Goodnight, Princess," and walked out of the room.

"Goodnight," Star replied and watched as his shadow disappeared.

June 27

"I've missed you," the familiar voice said as Star turned over.

She opened her eyes to see Jerick lying beside her in what felt like grass. *When did I go outside?* Star thought to herself looking into the morning sky. Its blue and yellow hues grazed across her face.

Jerick turned her face toward him and said, "Haven't you missed me?"

"I have, but it's not right for me to be here," said Star as she rose up and began to leave.

"Why isn't it right? You love me, don't you?" Jerick responded as he stood up and turned away from her.

"I don't really know what I feel right now. Jerick, please don't be mad with me. I just…" Star paused to figure out why it was so hard to tell him what she had learned about his past and that they couldn't be together.

Jerick was in front of her now, gazing into her eyes, coercing her to feel what he was feeling. "I've always known it was you. The ones before you didn't compare. You are just as Jaelyn once was. You are a star child, just like me. We belong together. Don't you know that? Can't you feel that?" he said, lifting her hand and placing it upon his heart.

Star looked down to see his hand on top of hers, moving with the beat of his heart.

Jerick came closer and brushed his lips across her ear. "I need you, Star. Come to me."

Suddenly, Star was taken away with his words, being pulled into a sea of emotions that she couldn't control.

Jerick pulled away as his words lingered in her ear.

"Jerick, wait, don't go," Star called out to him.

"Come be with me." Jerick turned and smiled, then continued to walk away.

Star followed behind him as her nightgown flowed in the breeze behind her.

✵ ✵ ✵

Jacy awoke to the creaking sound of the door opening. It was still dark outside, but his night vision pulled his eyes to the door swaying open in the night air. Jacy raced to the door to see Star wandering down the street.

He raced behind her and said, "Star, where are you going?"

Jacy pulled on her arm to stop her. Her eyes were glazed and focused into the night. Jacy realized that she was still asleep, so he shook her until her eyes fluttered and popped open wide.

"Where were you going?" Jacy yelled and then quieted his voice. "You scared me."

"I was…I was going to Jerick." Star began to cry as she brought her hands to her face to wipe her tears away.

"Why would you do that? You know what can happen if you give in to him."

"You don't know what it's like, Jacy," she cried embarrassingly. "I lose myself with him."

Jacy picked her up and said, "You're just out of it right now. Let me get you back to bed, Princess."

Star wrapped her arms around his shoulders and tucked her head into his neck. "I'm too afraid to go back to bed."

Jacy grinned. "If you don't get enough sleep, you won't be able to stay up late tonight for the bonfire. You'll need your energy with this bunch."

Star smiled, and Jacy took her inside. He walked up the stairs without making a sound. Even though Star was still upset, she noticed that the stairs didn't creak. They always made a sound when she went up and down them. The door to her new room swung open, and Jacy put her on the bed. She wiped her face again and slid beneath the sheets.

He sat down beside her and said, "Do you think you'll be all right?"

Star remembered her mother asking her the same question and how she wished she had stayed. She didn't want to be alone, but at the moment, she just wanted her mother. She couldn't call her because she didn't know if there was a time difference, and her mom could still be asleep, or awake, enjoying her day without her.

Instead she just replied, "I'll be fine. Thanks." She could see from the slight glare in the room that Jacy gave her a slight nod and stood up.

"Well, goodnight."

"Goodnight, Jacy."

He closed the door behind him, and Star rolled over, clutching her pillow. Tears slowly rolled down her cheek and onto her pillow. She missed her mom, she missed being at home, and she was only one day in her 365-day sentence.

✷ ✷ ✷

"I hope you got enough sleep last night because we're going to need your help." Kaya smiled watching Star walk down the stairs twirling her hair in her hands. "We're having a cookout tonight for you, but that doesn't mean you can't help," she laughed.

"Yeah, Jacy told me about it, but he didn't say it was for me. I don't want you to go through all of that trouble."

"There's no trouble at all," Ruth chimed in as she walked around the corner. "Would you like something to eat for breakfast?"

"Yes, please."

Kaya sat down to the table with her and began to eat her breakfast with Chenoa. Her eyes began to ask the question before the words could escape her mouth. "When did Jacy tell you? He left early this morning, and we didn't decide to do it until today."

Star sat puzzled and embarrassed at the same time. Obviously Jacy hadn't told her about last night. "Um, I think he mentioned it when he was getting his clothes last night for bed."

"Oh," said Kaya, putting a spoonful of cereal in her mouth.

Star felt relieved that she didn't question her further. Ruth placed cereal and toast in front of Star and sat down beside her. "This is your home now as well. So I want you to feel free to go in the fridge, kick up your feet, and come and go as you please. Even if it is just down the street." She smiled.

"Okay," Star replied and dug into her morning meal.

"So, what did you guys do when I went to bed?" asked Kaya.

"Oh, we just watched another movie, and then I went off to bed."

"I want to watch TV, Mommy," Chenoa blurted out as food circled around in her mouth.

"Don't talk with your mouth full. That's not ladylike," Kaya said, wiping her mouth.

✷ ✷ ✷

People were all over the place. Star was happy to be occupied in the kitchen with Ruth, Kaya, Stephen's mom, Ladon, and Poe's mom,

Leakesh. They were sisters who'd married into the Night Howlers. They looked alike, but they weren't twins. Leakesh was definitely the oldest. She would've taken over the kitchen if Ruth hadn't been there to maintain her control, something she seemed to have learned from being married to Jessie. Ladon was quiet, just like Stephen, only speaking when she really had something to say.

Star always enjoyed cooking with her mom, and this made her feel right at home. She was hesitant about coming downstairs at first, but her mom had been able to give her a nudge and a little confidence that she could just fit right in. She had gotten off of the phone with her mom just before everyone began to arrive. She was very happy that she had taken her mother's advice, but she could tell that she didn't quite make her mother happy when she'd told her about the dream. She was still a little shaken from both of her dreams now that she knew that it was all real, but she assured her mother that nothing was getting past her guardian.

Jacy tumbled into the kitchen with Stephen to check on the progress of dinner. Star couldn't understand how two guys that big could fit through the same door. The doors there seemed to have been raised and widened to fit the people who lived there. Jacy was bigger than Stephen, and they both looked like grown men, but Stephen was only a couple of months younger than Jacy.

Jacy came over to the table and grabbed a carrot.

"Hey!" Kaya shouted. "Your hands aren't clean."

Jacy shrugged his shoulders and walked over to Star, who was chopping onions. "You're always crying. I'm going to have to make sure I keep a close eye on you."

"I'm only crying because of the onions," Star laughed. She finished chopping the last bit of them and put the knife down. She leaned over to Jacy and whispered, "Whose idea was it for the party?"

"It was mine. I thought it would cheer you up."

"I'm okay. Really I am. I didn't need a party." She walked over to the sink and washed her hands.

"No worries," replied Jacy. He walked to her side and peered around her shoulder, chomping the last of his carrot. "Besides, this way you can meet everyone." Jacy smiled and left with Stephen, who had stolen something to eat as well.

✡ ✡ ✡

As the night went on, the party moved outside to enjoy the coolness of the evening air. It was amazing how much food came out of the kitchen, but even more so how much everyone ate. Stephen's dad, Ben, was there, as well as Cody's dad, Jack. There were so many other people Star met that night, but she couldn't remember all of their names. Poe's dad, Leroy, came late because of work to greet Star, and other family and friends came to say hello. Star still felt like a stranger, but found comfort in Chenoa, who seemed to have become attached to her hip.

Even though it was getting late, Chenoa didn't seem to tire. She asked Star to come outside and play. "Spin me again," she begged Star, jumping up and down.

"Okay," Star responded, picking her up by her hand and foot, swinging her up and down.

"Look at me! I'm a shooting star!" the little girl screamed out.

Star slowed down and let the little girl go in reaction to her comment. She whispered with a shaking voice to her, "Go to Mommy, okay?"

Tears began to well in Stars eyes as she looked around for a place to be alone. She couldn't go into the house because she would have to pass by several people to get upstairs, and she couldn't go in the front of the house because the majority of the pack was up there. She went to the only other place she was allowed to go. She made her way through the trees and dropped to the ground. She stared at the moon through an opening in the trees and continued to cry. She covered her face, hoping that her covered eyes would block her from the emotions that swirled in her mind. Suddenly Star felt someone beside her, someone warm over her, removing her hands from her face.

Jacy looked into her eyes, questioning her actions without mentioning his thoughts.

"I'm sorry," she sniffled. "I just wanted to be alone."

"What happened that made you get upset?"

"Shooting star."

"Shooting star, I don't understand."

"My dad used to call me that. He would throw me into the air and call me his shooting star. I hadn't heard it in a while, and when Chenoa said it, I just couldn't help it."

"How long has it been since he's been gone?" Jacy asked as his head still eclipsed the moon and his sympathetic eyes focused on hers.

"It's been almost three years."

"We need to get back before people start looking for us. I know what can cheer you up." Jacy stood up and pulled Star up to his chest. "I have one word for you: s'mores." Jacy smiled and pulled Star back through the opening to the woods. He turned to Star before they reached the crowd of people feasting and playing. "Do you need to wipe your nose in my shirt before we get back?"

"Gross." Star smiled and made a sour face. "No thank you."

July 10

I'm finding it easier and easier to fit in, Star thought as she doodled in her notebook and listened to her music. She still missed her mother and wanted to go home, but she was beginning to like it there. Suddenly, Chenoa stood in front of her, with Bear, wiping her little red nose.

Star pulled out her earplugs and said, "What's up, Chenoa?"

"Uncle Jace is going to the store, and he won't let me go with him."

"Well, if it makes you feel any better, I can't go either."

"Will you play with me?"

"Sure, what do you want to play?"

"Tea party."

"Don't bug her, Tweety," Jace said to Chenoa from the doorway.

Star laughed. "What did you call her?"

"Tweety. Doesn't she look like Tweety Bird from the cartoon? Especially when she cries."

Star smiled and replied, "She does. But she's not bugging me. We were just about to play tea party." She rolled off of the bed. "Besides, the way I see it, she shouldn't suffer alone."

"Oh, don't be so melodramatic. Kaya should be home from work soon, and Dad brews a mean pot of tea, right, Chenoa? Why don't you go and see what he's doing?" He leaned down and said to her, "I've got something to show Star."

Chenoa bought his ploy and went to find her grandfather.

"I thought you were going to the store?"

"Technically, Stephen was going to the store. My dad is down at Grandpa's house, but by the time Chenoa finds out, we'll be gone," Jacy laughed and grabbed Star's hand.

They made their way out the back door and into the woods. The sun was beaming down rays, as the clouds were on hiatus for the day.

"Where are we going?" Star asked as she felt her legs wobble beneath her.

"I have to show you something. Don't worry, we're almost there," he turned and said with a grin.

They walked into an open area in the woods that had tall trees encasing them like a circle with logs that copied them on the grassy floor below. There stood Poe, Cody, and Stephen, who was holding a brown paper bag that was stuffed to the brim with what looked like potato chips.

"Hey, cuz." Cody waved as the others waved in unison. Star waved with her free hand as Jacy released her other hand.

"We thought that it was time for you to see what we are." Jacy smiled as he walked backward toward the others. "We're going to need for you to turn around for a minute. I must warn you, though, we won't be able to speak with you after we change, and it may be a good idea if you don't scream."

Star rolled her eyes and turned around with her arms folded across her chest. She began to hear them take off their clothes and then what sounded like a blocks of ice crackling when they melt and the rustling of leaves. She felt a nudge on her shoulder and turned around. When she turned, a large snout pulled away from her. The large wolf joined the three other wolves who stood behind him and stood up on his hind legs. Star was shocked at how big they were. She had known that they had the capability to change into wolves, but they morphed into giant beings who tripled the size of a regular wolf and stood on their hind legs like men. They looked like something straight out of a horror film with their sharp teeth gleaming through their long snouts and their muscles that looked like they tightened with their every move. Jacy was obvious. His jet-black coat stood out from the rest. Star slowly walked to him as he lowered down on all fours to allow Star to brush the side of his cheek.

"Jacy?"

He nodded in agreement.

Star smiled and put her finger to her mouth. "Let me see, which one is Stephen?"

Jacy stepped aside, and Star walked over to the three remaining wolves. One stood with a red coat, the next was light brown with streaks of gray riddling his body, and the last had a coat of gray and white mixed and a white streak that went down the back of his head like a Mohawk. She pointed to the gray-and-white wolf and said, "Cody?"

The black wolf shook his head as if to say no.

"Okay, maybe not." She laughed. Star looked closer and said, "Are you Stephen?"

He came closer with a light growl and nodded yes.

"I should've known by your hair," she laughed. Stephen's hair was cut short like the others', but it was a little longer on the top so that he could style it in a tiny Mohawk.

The last two stood waiting to see if she could figure out their identities. She stood standing in between Jacy and Stephen with one hand on her hip and the other on her chin, tapping it with her finger. She thought of Cody's youthful personality and Poe's more eccentric demeanor. She pointed to the brown wolf and said, "Cody?"

The wolf ran over and licked her.

Star quickly wiped her face saying, "Cody, that was gross!" Jacy shot him a glance, and Cody nudged Star.

Jacy turned to Star and nudged her with his nose to turn around. Star figured that they wanted to change back. She turned again to allow them time to transform back and turned when she felt a hand on her shoulder.

"That was awesome." She grinned and shook her head. "Does it hurt when you do that?"

"No, not anymore. We've been doing this since we were five. At first you don't know what's going on because your body heat rises and your bones begin to ache, but we were warned that it would happen, so it's not such a shock."

"Were you guys that big when you were five?" Star asked.

Stephen walked over and answered, "We look like regular wolves at that age. As we grow older, we get bigger."

"And hairier," Poe said, tussling his hand through his hair.

Cody had joined them and was shocked that Star hadn't screamed. "I thought for sure you were going to scream or pass out," he laughed.

"Well, I wasn't scared, so no worries there. I am, however, in need of a bath." Star smiled as she wiped the side of her face that he'd licked again.

They sat around until nightfall, scarfing down the snacks that Stephen had picked up from the store and talking. Star learned that though the five of them were all different, they all had to share the same burden that had been placed on them centuries before they had even existed. The burden, however, didn't impact them at that moment. They were enjoying themselves just like people their age did. Poe and Cody were the clowns of the group. They weren't pleased until you were left with a smile on your face. Jacy was somewhat quiet and composed as usual. He barely spoke, but you could see that his mind was running, thinking about what he wanted to say, but he hardly ever said it. Something Star had also noticed was that Stephen was Jacy's right hand. He followed Jacy's every move when they were together. He was like Jacy in so many ways, but you could see that Jacy held something greater in him. He was the one who kept them together, stable, and focused. Even while sitting in the middle of the forest, Jacy was in charge.

"So what can you guys do besides turning into wolves?"

"Well, we're really fast and have the esteemed pleasure of guarding you," Jacy joked.

Cody chimed in, "We're also able to rip your guy into shreds. It doesn't kill him, but it's really hard to be put back together when we scatter him all over the place. It's only happened once, I guess centuries ago. If he can't find the pieces, he has to reabsorb the pieces from the Earth. It takes a while for him to come back, and he screams like a baby when he's pulled apart." He smiled.

Jacy shot him a glance that made Cody shut up instantly.

"My guy? Do you mean Jerick? He's not my guy. Technically, I've never even met him." Suddenly Star felt like she was the one being questioned. Was he her guy? And if he wasn't, why did she blush at the thought?

"I think it's time for real food," Jacy mentioned as he rubbed his stomach and stood up as if he hadn't seen the look on Star's face.

"I agree. I can hear Stephen's stomach all the way over here," Poe laughed.

They all got up and headed toward the house. Poe and Cody went home, but Stephen stayed behind because his mother and father had joined the family for dinner.

Kaya met them at the door with her hands on her hips. "Where have you guys been? I've been looking for you."

"We were just out back, about a mile away," Jacy whispered.

She walked over, grabbed Star's arm, and pulled her into the kitchen as Stephen and Jacy followed the aroma in the air from the dinner that had already been ravished on the table. "So what were you guys up to?" Kaya asked as she spooned food on a plate for Star.

"Oh, they just showed me their other side. Um, I guess you can call it their wolf forms." Star laughed because she didn't know what to call the wolf being that took over their bodies.

"Isn't it cool? I wish I could do it. It would've definitely been helpful when I had my C-section."

"Why couldn't you be one of them?"

"Only guys carry the wolf gene. So I'm just a regular old human, but I guess the upside of it is that we don't get sick," Kaya replied as she waved her hand in the air.

They walked over to the kitchen table and sat down. "Never?" Star asked.

"Well, not until we get pregnant. That's one thing we can't get away from," she smirked. "Morning sickness is a normal course of life, I guess."

Star spooned food in her mouth and asked, "What were you talking about before, when you said it would've helped with giving birth?"

"They may seem soft, but they are rock solid and can take pain much better than us. Jacy and I used to play around when we were younger, but that only lasted until he was about six or so. His play taps turned into a ton of bricks. It takes time for them to learn how to handle their newfound strength after they first shift. It was weird at first, having a little brother that you once gave piggyback rides to, or tricked out of his desserts, turn into the one that could pick you up or became smarter overnight. The change affects all of us in some way, I guess. I think what really made me realize that he was no longer just my little brother but a member of the pack was when he ran into the kitchen and Mom had just turned around with a knife in her hand. It grazed his cheek, but before Mom could even wipe the blood away, it had already healed. Between my stretch marks and suture line, I wish that was the one trait I had picked up instead of not getting sick."

"Great, Kay, you just ruined my dinner!" Jacy shouted, and he threw his fork onto the plate.

"I could never ruin your dinner. You eat everything."

"That's true," Jacy replied. He sat down to the table, picked up his fork, and continued eating.

✲ ✲ ✲

Star had grown accustomed to helping Jacy clean up the kitchen after dinner, so now he would give her the option to rinse or load. Star always chose rinse, but he always left the option open. Stephen sat at the table, waiting for Jacy to finish.

"So you guys aren't immortal, but you can rejuvenate yourselves?"

"Yeah, unfortunately we can't live forever," Jacy replied as a hint of doubt lingered in the air.

Star noticed the way he said it, but she didn't pressure him for more. She had just eaten until her stomach wouldn't take any more, and she felt really tired. After they were finished, she headed up to bed as Stephen and Jacy headed off to his makeshift bedroom in the living room.

Star called her mom to say goodnight and thumbed through her photo album. She had finally built up the courage to let it all in. She missed her mother's warm smile and their talks over ice cream and cookies. It wasn't like the way she missed her dad, because she knew he wasn't coming back. It was harder because her mother was somewhere within her grasp, but she couldn't be with her. She put the book on the nightstand, lay down and pulled the covers under her chin. She looked out the window until the stars began to fade into thin lines of darkness.

August 22

Every day that went by seemed to last longer and longer. Today started out just like all the rest. Star went downstairs to eat breakfast and watch movies while Jacy worked on the truck with his dad. She ate lunch with Ruth and Chenoa and then headed up to her room. She was stuck in the house, but happy to be away from the blazing sun. She sat wondering what was going on in the world as it passed her by. She felt like she was at home, gazing out of her window, wishing she could be a part of it, but there weren't people walking by with their dogs or driving by, only the woods that called out to her with their wavering leaves. Star opened her sketch pad, thumbing through the empty pages that still needed to be filled. She stopped at her last entry and began to write instead of draw. She wrote to her father how she missed his laughter and the way she could talk to him about anything. How he would love the Long Feathers and would be happy at how strong she was being. She turned the page and began to sketch, popping in her earbuds to block out the rest of the world that continued to exist without her.

Star dozed off, but was woken by her new alarm clock. Chenoa sat in front of her, holding Bear, tapping her on her face. "Wake up, Star. Grandma said it's time to eat," she said as she hopped off the bed and ran out of the room.

Star rubbed her eyes and went to the bathroom to wash up before dinner. She made her way downstairs as Kaya and Ruth set the food on the table. Jacy and Jessie were already sitting down, guiding the food to the table with their eyes. Jacy looked up when he noticed Star sitting.

"Did you have a nice nap? I think I heard you snoring all the way down here," he laughed and handed her the biscuits.

"Ha, ha, ha , very funny," Star jokingly laughed.

"Don't eat too much. We're having dessert by the fire tonight," Jacy replied, leaning toward her and smiling.

✵ ✵ ✵

They walked out into the field behind the house. Star wasn't sure where they were going, but didn't bother to ask since she always seemed to be in the dark. As they continued to walk, Star began to recognize some of the layout. They were going to the circular field where the pack had revealed themselves to her. When they arrived, the fire was already raging. Poe was there with his parents, as well as Stephen and Cody. Grandpa Joe sat across from the opening, waving Jessie over, while the pack waved for Jacy.

"You can come over here with us, girls," Kaya said, pulling Star's arm. Stephen's sister, Cadee, was sitting with her mom and Poe's little sister, Myra. She was very hyper for a six-year-old, but she had probably gotten worse because of all of the sugar she had running through her. Still, she didn't compare to Chenoa, who was almost four.

"Here you go, honey," Leakesh said, handing Star a marshmallow on a stick.

"Thank you," Star replied as she turned and headed to the fire with the other girls.

After they had their fill of chocolate and graham crackers, everyone settled down around the fire. Star sat down with Kaya, and Chenoa curled up with her. Jacy stayed on the other side with the guys. Grandpa Joe still sat where he did when they had arrived in the field. Jessie sat beside him, along with Ben, Leroy, and Jack.

Star sat, curious, as Grandpa Joe began to speak. "It's been a while since we've gotten together, but I felt it was time to tell the young one her purpose for joining us."

Grandpa Joe looked at Star. She felt like everyone else's eyes were on her as well. His, however, held her stare, and she began to question his statement. Hadn't she already known what her purpose was? What else had been hidden from her?

"I think that Jessie can tell the story better than I." He turned and looked to him to begin.

Jessie began just as directed and took control of Stare's stare. "Jerick had roamed the Earth for years not knowing when his beloved would return. Unfortunately for him, he possessed his father's bitterness and jealousy, which only grew worse every day that went by. After he had learned about the coming of the Fourth Star, he begged his father Aakesh to help him because his time was running out. Aakesh knew that he had nothing Earthly to offer his son for assistance, but if he were to prosper in his plight, something had to be done. Aakesh gave the one thing that tied him to his son, the gift of entering one's dreams."

Star gasped for air hearing what he had said. Jessie noticed, but he continued, "Jerick would be able to communicate with the girl, but with doing so, he could no longer have contact with his father. Jerick, being the spoiled immortal that he had become, quickly took his father's gift and said good-bye to him forever.

"The Fourth Star, Beth, had already come to stay with us by that time, and had been here since her fifteenth birthday. It was thought that if she stayed away long enough, she would be too old for Jerick to be with her. She was free to roam around the reservation, but was still guarded. Her life only consisted of her studies, and her free time was spent with her guardians. They had spent so much time together that she eventually fell in love with one of them, Adam. Adam was smitten by the girl from the moment he saw her and she him. Their relationship was kept hidden until she was with child. Her parents found out about the affair and her pregnancy, so they removed her from our care saying that we corrupted her and used the legends as a way to steal their daughter from them. It was a different time then, and Adam, poor Adam, lost his love and his child. It was said that after the child was born, she was given to her aunt, and Beth was put into an institution because of her night terrors and wandering through the night.

"By the time Jerick had learned of her whereabouts, she was already gone. The pack tore him apart before he retreated with the limbs that remained intact. They kept her feelings about Adam a secret from him, knowing that his fight for her would not be won. He tried with all his might, using his gift as a way to lure her to him, but her heart was already Adam's."

Star's stomach lurched at the thought, as she had been unaware of her great-grandmother's fate and remembered her own recent stroll through the night.

Jacy looked over at her with his eyes focused on her. He knew what she may have been thinking.

Jessie moved his gaze from Star and stared at the fire, continuing with his story. "Jerick was also unaware of the child because Beth was sedated and kept locked away. He continued to visit her in her dreams until he figured out her location. When he found her, she was almost forty years old and unable to withstand the power that was her birthright. The human body can't withstand the blood of Lucero alone. His human descendants and their companions have all but perished. Those that remain are still here on borrowed time. All but the last Starfire, her days are numbered. She would meet her end on the day that marks her eighteenth year of her life."

Jacy looked up at Star, who was sitting across from him. He could see her wiping her eyes, trying to hide behind her hair. She then repositioned a sleeping Chenoa on her lap to cover her face when she noticed Jacy watching her.

"Kaloy had learned of Jerick's failed attempt and that the gift that he had given to Aakesh out of pity was given to his son without his permission. Kaloy called forth the Sun King Paytah and decided that because Aakesh had helped his son, the same favor should be bestowed upon Starfire.

"Paytah created a dagger that was shaped from hundreds of stars mounted together to a point. The blade was given to an officer named Felix, created specifically to keep an eye on Star, to bring upon the Earth and remain as a secret guardian for the last of her kind. Lucero was summoned to see that the Night Howlers guarded the blade and the child only if Jerick came near. Due to his spoiled behavior and lack of humanity, his life would be taken if the blade was pierced through his heart. Aakesh was not to be told of its existence, and the child would be protected away from society so that her whereabouts were left unknown except for by her guardians. Lucero asked that because Aakesh was given communication to his son, that he also be able to give her a gift and that the last Starfire be given Jerick's immortality because of his actions.

"Kaloy agreed with his wish, but gave warning that even though she would be granted immortality, she could never return home. Lucero wasn't happy to hear that she couldn't return, but was satisfied with his ruling. Paytah released his servant to Earth so that he could carry out their wishes.

"Felix came to Grandpa Joe's father and asked for a place to hide the dagger until it was time for the last Starfire to receive its calling. He agreed that it should be hidden in an area that wasn't touched by the sun, but near the reservation. A cave opening that hung upon a cliff nearby became the home of the only weapon that could kill Jerick if the last of Lucero's descendants chose to use it. He showed Felix the opening and followed as Felix found the perfect spot in the cave to hide the dagger. He reached into a bag that hung to the side of his hip, and from his mouth Felix blew out a burst of flames into the walls, which turned them into glass. The chief marveled at the structure as Felix pulled out the dagger that was wrapped in cloth and opened a metal box that beamed such a bright light that it caused him to look away. When he opened his eyes, a starlike being held the dagger in midair. Felix gestured for the chief to exit the area, and he knocked down the wall of dirt behind him to close it in. He then blew another gust of fire to make an imprint in the dirt with his fingers in the shape of a star.

"'This place must only be known to the Night Howlers. Its safety and secrecy is as important as those of the duties already bestowed upon them.' That still holds true to this day," Jessie said as he now looked directly at Star. "The secret will remain with us until you are ready to take hold of your destiny."

Star felt like the world was caving in on her. All she wanted to do was run away. The toddler lying in her arms was the only thing keeping her grounded. This whole time they had been keeping yet another secret from her. They knew that her mother's life would soon end and that even the year to come was not promised to her.

Kaya put her hand on Star's shoulder and asked, "Do you want me to take Chen from you?"

Without saying a word, Star handed her the child, and Kaya walked away. Star still sat while her mind swam in what she felt was betrayal. Jacy sat down next to her, watching the others retreat home. They saw the toll the story had on Star and thought it best not to bother her. Star could no longer hold her anger and let her body swim in her tears. She wrapped her arms around her legs and drilled her head into her arms. She felt more alone than the first day she had gotten there. Jacy sat with her until she stopped sobbing and stroked her hair to make her look up.

"Please go away." Her voice cracked.

"I'm not going to leave you out here by yourself, and besides, you don't know the way back anyway." Jacy sat silently. "Look, I'm sorry. I thought that you were ready to hear…"

"Ready to hear what, that my mom is going to die soon or that I'm going to die before I've even been able to live?" Star stood up and stormed away.

"Wait, where are you going?" Jacy called out and grabbed her arm. "You have to understand that this is all for you and that none of us want you to die. Immortality is right around the corner for you. You just have to reach out for it."

"So that I can watch my mother and everyone that I meet die? Why would I want to live a life like that? A life full of tears and loneliness is not fun. I should know." Star felt anger course through her veins, a feeling that she had never felt before.

Jacy didn't utter one word as he noticed a flicker of light in Star's eyes and watched her body slink to the ground. Jacy lifted her from the ground, tapping her on her face, and called out to her, but she didn't respond.

Star woke just as Jacy reached the house. "Wh-What happened?" she said as she wiped her forehead.

"You passed out," Jacy replied nervously, holding her in his arms.

Star realized where she was and asked to be put down.

"Are you sure? I can carry you to bed."

"No, please, I don't want anyone to know what happened."

Jacy looked down at her while he put her on her feet. "My father and all of the other Night Howlers are always aware of what's going on. We can hear each other's thoughts and see them just as clearly as if they were our own. My father is waiting for us to come in as we speak."

More secrets, Star thought to herself. She turned, trying to hide her anger, and walked into the house the minute Jessie opened the door. "Are you all right, dear?"

"I'm fine. I just want to go to bed," she replied and walked upstairs.

"I'm sorry, Dad. I thought she was ready."

"She is ready. She just needs time to wrap her head around it all. You need to help her realize that she has a reason to live."

"But I'm not sure if I can do that, Dad. I…"

Jessie stopped him before he spoke the words. "Don't forget, you have a duty to uphold first and foremost. That's your first priority. Don't let this be like the last time."

Jacy understood what his father was saying and knew that his love for Starfire would have to wait. Only, after what they had put her through tonight, she may never want to speak with him again.

August 23

Star lay in her covers not wanting to face the day or the people who surrounded her. She wanted to pack her things and run away, but she knew that they would catch her before she had even gotten to Grandpa Joe's house. She even thought about Jerick, the man everyone kept her away from, but was he really so bad? He wanted to be with her, and right now she wanted to be with him. With him, she had no worries, no lies, and she wasn't alone.

Suddenly there was a knock at the door. Kaya walked in. "Is it okay if I come in?"

"Sure," Star answered as she sat up in the bed.

Kaya sat beside her and whisked her cropped bang from her eye. "I know that yesterday was kind of rough for you, but you had to find out sooner or later. Don't be mad at Jacy. He thought that telling you would give you a sense of belonging and something to look forward to."

"Belonging?"

"Yeah, family, silly. Weren't you listening? Your great-grandmother had a baby with one of the pack. Cody's great-grandfather was Adam."

"We're cousins?"

Kaya nodded. "But even if you weren't related to them, you're still family to us." She held out her arms, and Star lifted into them.

"Thank you, Kaya."

"Now get up. It's almost lunch time, and Jacy's been biting on his fingers all morning. Promise me that you won't be too harsh." Kaya smiled.

✿ ✿ ✿

Star took a shower, slipped on one of her dresses, and went downstairs. Her flip-flops announced her entrance as she scoped the room for Jacy.

Kaya figured what Star was looking for and said, "He's out back." She pointed out the back door and continued reading her magazine.

Star looked at the cover of the magazine, trying to find the postage sticker. Maybe she could finally find out where she was, but it had already been torn off. Feeling guilty of her actions last night and for her thoughts that morning, Star grabbed a banana off of the counter and picked at it, trying to think of what to say. She finished eating and went outside to find Jacy talking to Stephen. The deck had built-in seats that wrapped around it, like in a sauna, and a walkway that led out into the woods.

Stephen saw her coming and had begun to make his retreat, but stayed long enough to tell Star hello.

"Hi," Star said bashfully. "You don't have to leave."

"Oh, I was heading out anyway. See you guys later."

Jacy still stood with his back to Star and didn't turn around.

"Jacy, I wanted to apologize for how I acted last night. None of this is your fault, and I took it out on you. It wasn't fair of me to do that. I'm really sorry."

Jacy turned, shocked at her statement. "You're apologizing to me?" He shook his head. "Last night was my fault. I should've given you more time to adjust to the situation. Look, let me make it up to you."

"You don't have to. I still don't feel like this is your fault." Star shrugged.

Jacy stretched out his hand and said, "Come with me."

Star obliged and gave him her hand. He held on leading her into the forest behind the house. Usually when she was out there, the night covered the beauty that lay in the trees that hung bountifully and masked the daylight sky. Butterflies fluttered nearby as they awakened the sleeping grass. Woodland creatures scampered and hid when they heard them walking by.

"I didn't realize how nice it was out here."

"You should get out of the house more often." Jacy turned and smiled. They made their way to an open field that wasn't as big as the one they were in before, but was still filled with the same beauty that encased the rest of the fields.

"What are we doing out here?" Star asked as Jacy let go of her hand.

"Have you ever ridden a horse before?"

"That's a weird question," she replied, giggling curiously.

"I'm serious. Have you?"

Star thought back to a trip she once took to the fair with her parents. She remembered holding on to her red balloon in one hand and her cotton candy in the other. Her father carried her on his shoulders and held on to her feet. He pulled her off of his shoulders and took her treats, then gave them to her mother. At first she didn't know where he was taking her, until she saw the ponies. She remembered her father lifting her up on one. It was brown with white spots all over it. She could remember the strong smile on his face when he leaned over and told her not to be afraid. They went around in a circle like they were on a merry-go-round. Waving whenever she came around to her parents, it became one of her fondest memories of them together.

"I rode a pony once." She smiled, knowing that wasn't the same as riding a horse.

"Okay." Jacy laughed and leaned in to say, "Do you want me to give you a ride?"

Star stood puzzled at his question.

"I mean with me as a wolf," Jacy said, taking her hand in his. "All you have to do is hold on tight and don't be afraid."

With her father's words echoing in her ear, she nodded yes. Star turned around, knowing that Jacy needed to undress before he turned. His face rubbed against her shoulder to turn around. She smiled at his appearance and ran her hand along the side of his face. Jacy lifted his head and held out his left paw to help lift her on his back. Star kicked off her pink flip-flops and climbed on top of the large wolf, swinging her leg around his body. Her heart began to beat so hard that even Jacy noticed and grunted in his throat as to laugh. She wrapped her hands in strands of his fur and dug her legs into his side.

"I'm ready," she whispered into his ear, and he charged off, leaving his clothes and the quiet field behind them.

Her laughter echoed throughout the forest. She had never felt so alive before. Her hair flowed in the wind, dancing with her dress beneath. She had been so afraid of getting up that day, but if she had known that this awaited her, she would've gotten up at sunrise.

Star recognized the field upon their return. Jacy's clothes still lay in a pile on the ground, with her shoes, in the still forest awakened by Star's laughter. She slid down his back and onto his paw with a smile that Jacy had never seen before.

She leaned over and kissed him on his muzzle. "Thank you."

September 18

The rustling of little feet grazed across the floor while Star watched *Pretty in Pink*. Chenoa walked into the living room and sat on the couch with her. They had grown into couch buddies who took over Jacy's bed almost every day after breakfast. Jacy was out back talking with his father, while Ruth was still upstairs. About midway through the movie, Jacy joined the two on the couch, and Jessie opened his arms for his morning hug from Chenoa.

"Good morning, Grandpa!"

"How's my big girl?"

"Fine, Grandpa. Are you going to watch TV with me?"

"Not right now, but maybe later, okay?"

"Okay!" Chenoa replied and wiggled out of his arms. She crawled back onto the couch between Star and Jacy, snuggling with her bear.

"I'll see guys later. I have some errands to run," Jessie mentioned just before he walked out the door.

"So what do you girls have planned after the movie goes off?"

Chenoa smiled and said, "I want to go swimming." Kaya had bought her an inflatable pool that she asked to swim in every day, but it wound up being only once or twice a week.

"No plans here," Star replied.

"I thought that maybe we should go and visit Grandpa Joe for a little while."

"Sounds cool to me." "How about you?" asked Star looking down at Chenoa.

"I guess so. Can Bear come?"

"Sure, why don't you go and get her dressed?" Jacy said as he lifted her off of the couch. "*Pretty in Pink* again, huh?"

"Yeah, it's my favorite!" Star replied.

"Do you think that you can watch Chenoa at Grandpa Joe's for a little while? I have to go somewhere."

"Where are you going?" Star smiled curiously.

"Unfortunately, if I told you, I would have to kill you." Jacy smiled and grabbed her head for a noogie.

"I can't breathe," she mumbled, and Jacy let go. They wrestled until Chenoa came in the room.

"We're ready!" she shouted, holding up a fully dressed Bear.

"What about your shoes, Chen? You'll need shoes, too, if you're coming with us," Jacy laughed.

"I guess I better go and get my shoes on as well." Star went upstairs and pulled on her Converses. She met up with Chenoa at the stairs and came down holding her hand just as Jacy stopped the movie.

"Let's go, Uncle Jace," Chenoa said, handing Bear to Star. She grabbed his hand and walked out the door. Star followed behind.

They walked down the street, swinging Chenoa in between them. Grandpa Joe met them on the porch. The light green house sat closer to the road and was smaller than the Long Feathers' but had a porch out front. It looked warm and welcoming, just like Grandpa Joe. The steps creaked when they stepped on them, alerting others to their presence.

"Hello girls. Jacy."

"Hi," Chenoa wailed as she jumped into his arms.

Jacy turned to Star and told her that he would back as soon as he could. Star nodded and said, "Ok, I'll see you later."

"Bye, Uncle Jace!" Chenoa waved as he walked away.

"So what do you girls want to do? I have some puzzles in there, and coloring books. I haven't had to take care of a teen in a while, so I'm sorry I don't have anything better for you to do. It was kind of a last-minute thing."

Star laughed. "It's okay. I like puzzles." Star walked into the house behind them inspecting all that she saw. Its furniture was reminiscent of an elderly woman's touch. The rose lace curtains hung in the windows, and quilted blankets covered the couch. Wooded floors flooded throughout the house just as they did at the Long Feathers'. Star noticed on the mantel of the fireplace a ceramic jar with faded colors and a crack on the side. *Is that the jar?* Star thought to herself.

Grandpa Joe smiled as he followed her eyes and could see that she knew what it was. He led them to the kitchen, where he pointed out the corner that was the home of puzzle boxes and newspapers.

"Jacy was supposed to come and clean up, but he's been preoccupied these days," he laughed.

"I can do it for you," Star replied.

"No, no, that's okay."

"It's kind of my fault he hasn't been able to do it, so please let me."

✡ ✡ ✡

Jacy made his way out past the clearing and met up with his father, Poe, Stephen, and Cody.

"I can smell him coming," Jessie said as he began to transform. His smell blended with the earth, but it was a smell the Night Howlers had grown used to. It was like earth, wind, and fire all rolled into one, stronger than the elements on their own. The rest of the pack followed suit, shedding off their jeans and T-shirts, unraveling into massive beings. "Remember what we taught you. He's fast, and this time he's fighting for much more."

Jerick had grown angry because he was still unable to get to Star. He had figured out that Star was being held by the Night Howlers, but he wouldn't allow them to stop his last chance to be with her. Jessie, Jacy, and Stephen met him before he could step foot on their land. He stood, knowing the fierceness of their bite, but he had to try. He stood ready to strike, but saw the anxiety in the black wolf.

"You," he called out. "I recognize you. She dreams about you, but it's me she comes after. It's because of you that I can't come visit her. I bet, even now, it's me that her mind wonders about."

Jacy growled, but held his stance.

"He's just trying to distract you. Don't let him, Jacy," said Jessie with his inner voice.

Jerick began to pounce from side to side, trying to make his way between the tight *V* formation they had made to block his path. He jumped and maneuvered his way toward Poe, but Stephen and Jessie pounced in front of him. Jacy joined in the fight as Cody stood to see where he could fit in. They tore at his flesh, and when pierced, sand fell from its openings. Poe found his way in and tore away half of his skull while Jacy went in for the jugular and ripped his arm from his body just below his neck.

Jerick screamed out in pain. His limbs littered the forest floor. Only a third of his body still remained. He crawled over and pulled his arm over to him as his body continued to seep sand like an hourglass. "You may have won," he choked out and coughed, "but I will have her."

Jerick cowardly sped away, leaving a trail of dust behind him. His remaining body parts disintegrated, and the Night Howlers howled at their victory, but knew that it was only short-lived, because he would be back soon.

✲ ✲ ✲

Star and Chenoa heard the howling in the woods and turned to Grandpa Joe for its meaning. "Oh, they're just at one of their council meetings right now."

"Why aren't you there?"

Grandpa Joe was caught off guard by her question but quickly thought of an answer. "I don't bother myself with a lot of the Night Howlers' business anymore. Besides, I can stay right here and still know what's going on," he said while pointing to his head.

"So what happened?" she asked.

"Boy, you're full of questions. Usually it's this one over here that has me on my toes," he responded while pointing his thumb at Chenoa. "Jacy just won something, so he was howling at his victory." That answer was compliments of Cody, as Grandpa Joe couldn't come up with anything to say. He tried to change the subject, so he said, "Thanks for cleaning up the kitchen for me."

"You're welcome," Star replied, trying to piece together a puzzle on the kitchen floor. Chenoa moved the pieces like she was creating some other puzzle. They had been there for over an hour, and all she had to show for it were the edges.

An hour later Jacy came by to pick up the girls with a smile on his face that beamed like the morning sun.

"So what did you win?"

"Oh, I won twenty bucks from Cody. He bet me that you would have gone to the cave by now." Star stewed over Jacy's answer for a while. "You guys bet on me?"

"Don't be so sensitive. You can have the twenty if you want it."

"No thanks," Star replied, returning back to the puzzle she was cleaning up. Chenoa was already ready to go with Bear.

"It was nice having you guys here." Grandpa Joe waved and said good-bye as they walked outside.

They walked to the house without really saying a word. Jacy's comment lay heavy on Star's mind. They reached the house, and Jacy told Chenoa to go inside. Star watched her walk inside and then turned to Jacy.

"What's up?" Star questioned.

"Why haven't you asked to go yet?"

"Who said that was a life I wanted to live?" she replied defensively.

Jacy's face changed into something different. No longer did he express the glow that had just been there five minutes ago. "Why wouldn't you want to live this life? What's so bad about it that you would rather die than to live an eternity with…"

"An eternity alone! Everyone I know and love will die, and I will still be here. I don't want to die, but I don't want to live knowing that I took someone else's life either."

"Someone else? This isn't about you at all, is it? This is about him. You're in love with him, aren't you?"

"Please don't be upset with me. I don't know what I'm feeling right now. But I do know that it's not my choice whether someone lives or dies, no matter what they did in the past."

Jacy told her to go in the house, and he stormed off. Star couldn't go inside after what had just happened. She sat down on the porch and tried to wrap her mind around it. His reaction made her choke with guilt, but it wouldn't make her cry. What gave him the right to be upset about the choices she made? She ran her fingers through her hair and composed herself before she walked into the house. Star knew that the whole pack had seen what had just taken place, so she couldn't make eye contact with any of them. She went upstairs and closed the door behind her.

September 19

"Where are you? I can hear you, but I can't see you," Star called out to Jerick.

"I'm hurt. They…they tried to kill me."

"Who tried to kill you?"

"Please come to me. I need you."

✵ ✵ ✵

Jacy came into the house still displaying his defeated appearance. He walked into the kitchen and found Kaya cleaning up. "Thanks a lot for taking the night off when everyone was over," she said sarcastically. "Star took the night off too. What happened with you guys?"

"Nothing," Jacy responded. "Where is she?"

"Mom says that she's been upstairs since she came home. She didn't even come down for dinner. Seriously, what happened?"

"Later, Kaya," Jacy said, and he walked up to her room. The light was still on, and the door was slightly open. He knocked and slowly opened the door, but no one was there. The night air lingered in the room through the window that was still open. He walked over to the bed and saw Star's sketchbook lying on the bed with her pencil holding its latest page open. Jacy picked up the book and saw his face staring back at him. At the bottom of the page Star had written:

I keep upsetting him, but I did nothing wrong. I don't understand why he thinks I'm in love with Jerick. I don't even know what it feels like to be in love. I've never even been able to control my own life, and now I'm responsible for the fate of everyone. Why is he so upset about it anyway? After this is over, he can finally live his life the way that he wants to. I know that for the sake of mankind I can't be with Jerick, but if I can at least say good-bye to my mother, I'm okay with letting go.

Jacy closed the notebook, trying to figure out where she would be. He walked over to the door and looked down the hall, but there wasn't anyone in the bathroom. Kaya called out to him to see what was going on. "She's not up here," Jacy yelled.

Kaya had made it to the room and said, "What do you mean she's not up here? Dad would've known if she left."

Just then a breeze flowed through the window, catching Jacy's nose. "Lilacs," he said lightly to himself. He ran to the window and peered out of it to find Star walking toward the end of the roof. Her ponytail swayed in the wind as she stepped off. "Star!" he called out. "Star, no!"

Jessie saw his thoughts and ran outside just as she descended through the air and landed in his rock-hard arms. She gasped for air like she was underwater.

"Ow!" she cried out.

"Are you okay, honey?" Jessie asked the frightened girl.

"I feel like I've been hit by a ton of bricks."

"Let's get you upstairs," Jessie said just when Jacy had made it to the door.

Ruth was standing at her room door when Jessie took her back to her room. He asked Ruth to get Star some water and pain medication. "You're going to hurt for a little while, but it's better than you hitting your head on the pavement," he said as he laid her on the disheveled covers. Jacy had come into the room carrying blankets and a pillow. His father had instructed him to sleep in the room with her so that they wouldn't have another incident. "Remember our conversation, son. The purpose comes first."

Jessie turned to Star and said, "Jacy is going to bunk with you now. This way you won't get a chance to even get out of the window." He smiled and handed her the glass of water that Ruth had brought up along with the pain meds.

Star was in too much pain to be as apologetic as usual. She swallowed the pills and slid down into the bed with her body aching. Jacy laid his blankets down at the end of her bed and watched her fall asleep before he also began his slumber.

September 26

Days had passed, and Star had still felt a little sore. She wondered if it would have been better to just crack her skull or break a leg. She spent most of her time lying in bed, drawing, or reading her book, while Jacy moped around the house. She tried to tell him that Jerick made her go outside and that this was not his fault, but he still blamed himself. He barely spoke to her. The only words he spoke were "Goodnight, Princess" and "Good morning, Princess."

Star looked down at her bracelet that her mom had given her on her birthday. It made her think of her whenever she looked down at it. *If a tiny gift such as a bracelet can bring me such joy, what would make him happy?* she thought to herself.

She crawled off of the bed and went over to the closet, where her bag hung, holding the money that her mother had given to her. She hadn't touched it since the day she found it. The Long Feathers' provided her with everything she needed, so she never found a use for it. She knew that Jacy could hear anything she said, so she grabbed a piece of paper and a pen. She went downstairs, almost tripping over her long sweatpants, to find Kaya. She was in the kitchen talking with her mother and saw Star come down the stairs. Star motioned for her to come over. Growing fonder of the idea, a smile spread across her face. Star sat down on the step behind her, and Kaya followed suit.

"What's up? Are you going to hang out here with the rest of us today or stay in your cell?" she said, waving her hand up the stairs. "Between you and Jacy, I don't know who's worse."

"That's why I needed your help." Star gave her the paper, where she had already written her request: Jacy will hear you, so I wrote it down. I want to get him something to cheer him up. My mother gave me some money, so I want to use it on him.

Kaya smiled and wrote: Jacy doesn't need anything. She paused and then continued writing. He just needs time to get over what happened to you.

Star grabbed the paper and pen, shaking her head, and wrote: I know there's something I can do. Just tell me.

Kaya sighed and wrote: Buy hiking boots.

Star made a weird face and wrote: Okay. Just let me know how much.

Kaya nodded, and Star went back upstairs. Kaya watched her walk upstairs and shook her head, saying, "Kids today."

October 2

The weather had really begun to change as the air turned brisk and the leaves began to cascade down into piles of autumn mountains below. Now that her window was bolted shut, she couldn't feel the breeze from upstairs, but Star had always liked this time of year, when the trees changed colors and you were able to wear sweaters all the time. She had even picked up Ruth's habit of wearing one when she was around the pack. Star had also made some headway with Jacy, as he now spoke to her three times a day. He would ask Star if she needed anything, but that was it. Star resumed her kitchen duties, but she still couldn't get him to talk. The plates and forks made more of a sound than the two of them when they cleaned up the kitchen. Stephen would wait until after dinner to stop by. Even though he loved Ruth's cooking, he couldn't stomach the new quiet Jacy that only appeared around Star.

Kaya came home late from work that day. She worked part-time at a nearby diner. Her hours weren't always the same, but she never worked the late shift, so it was odd that she wasn't there for dinner. She came in carrying a bag and placed it on the table that Star had just wiped.

"Hey, I just cleaned that, you know."

"Oh, stop being such a sourpuss." Kaya smiled and pinched Star's cheek. "I have the gift you asked me to pick up."

"Kaya," Star said in a grim voice.

"No, you should do it now," Kaya said as she pulled out the box from the bag.

Jacy turned, resting himself along the counter. With a questioning look upon his face, he grinned and asked, "You got me something?"

Kaya smiled while she took off her coat and placed her hand on her hip. "Not you, her."

Star stood puzzled now at her comment. She opened the box and pulled out a pair of women's hiking boots.

"Kaya, those are for women. I told you to get him something."

Jacy smiled at the gesture.

"I did. You asked me what would make him happy."

"You said hiking boots."

"Yes, hiking boots for you so that you could go hiking and maybe pick up a certain dagger along the way. You can thank me later, little bro." She smiled and put the boots back in the box. "I'll take these up to your room," Kaya crooned as she collected her things and walked upstairs.

Star turned to hold on to the table so that she could steady herself and then wiped the section that Kaya had just placed the bag on. She felt Jacy come over and stand beside her.

"You're not happy about what she did, are you?"

"So you're talking to me now?" Star questioned him without looking up.

"I didn't know she was going to do that," he said with his warm breath brushing her brow.

"I know you didn't. It was my bright idea." Star turned around and placed that dishcloth on the sink.

"You don't have to do it if you don't want to," Jacy responded with his head hanging low.

Star turned and replied, "Will this make you happy?"

Jacy stood, still not knowing what to say, as the pack was in his head, telling him to say yes. He looked down and then back up at Star. "Your happiness, your life, is what makes me happy. If you don't want to live, if doing this doesn't make you happy, then I don't want you to do it."

His response threw her for a loop. They both stood in silence while she pondered a response. "Of course I want to live, and I...I am happy."

"No, you're not. I can hear you crying in the bathroom, even when the shower is running. I know you're not happy here, and that's what makes me unhappy. You have so many things that you can still do in life, but you're throwing it all away to save him." His dark eyes stared at her. He waited, longing for her to say something, anything.

How could she tell him that she didn't want to live forever because that would mean she would have to say good-bye to him too? This whole time she had thought about saying good-bye to her mother and how she would never see her father again, but it had just dawned on her that she didn't want to watch him die either. She brushed away the thought and came to the conclusion that if he could give up his life to protect her, then she could give up her selfishness and self-pity to make him happy.

"I'm not holding back to save him. I told you the reason why I didn't want to do it. But my reasons for doing it outweigh them now." She swallowed deeply and said, "So, when can we go?" She formed a smile that held no joy, but when Jacy came over and picked her up in a bear hug, her smile turned into pure delight.

October 3

Jacy rolled over, unable to sleep. He had been waiting years for today's activities, but he still felt like he wasn't prepared.

"You can do it, man," Poe said to him.

"I don't think that's what I'm having a problem with. It's getting harder and harder every day not to tell her how I truly feel."

"You won't let us down, Jacy. He'll come back for her, and we'll be ready. Then you can tell her."

"Okay, I'll wait, but I don't want any flak about my thoughts." He laughed inside. He quietly got up and rolled up his blankets. He walked over to the bed, where Star still slept peacefully. How he wanted to curl up beside her, brush the hair from her neck, and nestle his face in its place. *Soon,* he said to himself as he walked out of the room.

✧ ✧ ✧

"Wake up, sleepyhead," Kaya said, shaking Star's shoulder.

Star blinked and opened her eyes to see Kaya sitting in front of her. She sat up wiping her face, trying to focus her eyes on the clock to see what time it was. The bright red light said that it was 7:16. With a groggy voice, Star said, "I thought you had to work today?"

"There's no way I would miss this!"

Star smiled and asked, "Where's Jacy?"

"Oh, he's just as excited as I am. He's already packed a bag for lunch and made Mom get up early so that breakfast will be ready for you. It's going to be a long day, you know?"

"Well how far away is this place anyway?"

"If it were just Jacy, he could be back in an hour or two, but with you, it will be at least half a day's hike going. I took the liberty of picking you up a hat and some gloves the other day. I hope you like them. It's going to be cold out there after a while. Now get up. Jacy's waiting for you downstairs."

Star ran to the shower and returned to her room to get dressed. What would someone wear to go hiking? She pulled out a pair of jeans and a long-sleeve shirt. "I guess this will have to do," she said to herself. She walked over to the mirror, now not knowing what to do with her hair. She twisted it between her fingers, staring in the mirror, when she noticed Ruth walking into the room.

"Is it all right if I come in?"

Star nodded as she walked over to her.

"Looks like you're stuck. Do you want me to help?"

Star nodded again. She couldn't speak. The moment reminded her of the morning of her birthday, when her mother had come in to help.

"Today's a very important day for you. I know it hasn't been easy for you being here, but today is the first part of making it all worth it. I have no doubt that this is the best thing for you, but it's you that can't doubt the fact that you are an amazing person. I see that, and Jacy sees it as well. You have no idea the power you have and what you will soon possess. Just make sure you use it wisely," she said while giving Star a reassuring smile. "There, all finished."

Star looked in the mirror and saw a braid that cascaded across the top of her head and down her shoulder.

"Do you like it?"

"I do. Will you teach me how to do it one day?"

"Yes, I would love to after you turn eighteen." Ruth smiled and kissed her forehead.

✮ ✮ ✮

Jacy sat on the deck, waiting for Star to come out. Ruth made Star eat so much food that she thought that her stomach was going to burst. She just wanted to head back upstairs and hop back into bed, but she'd already promised Jacy that she would go, and even worse, Kaya had taken the day off in anticipation. She made her way outside wearing her new winter gear and her fuchsia jacket that she'd packed. The hat and gloves that Kaya had picked up for her were speckled with fuchsia, purple, black, and white. The gloves were actually mittens. Star didn't mind. They were warm, and that was all that counted as the cold air met her once she opened the door.

Jacy smiled and walked over to her. "Good morning, Princess. Are you ready to go?"

"As ready as I guess I'll ever be." She smiled as she closed the door behind her. "Is that all you're going to wear?" she asked, glancing at his wardrobe. Jacy wore a black hoodie, which was slightly unzipped to reveal a band T-shirt underneath, and jeans.

"Technically I don't even need this on." Jacy smiled and picked up his backpack. "Are you sure you don't want me to carry you? I heard you and Kaya talking earlier, and she's right. It would be a lot quicker."

"Wasn't it you that said I need to get out more often? Besides, the walk will do me some good. It seems like I was stuck in the bed for days."

"It was days. I'm going to have to get a new mattress when you leave," he laughed.

"Shut up!" she shouted and nudged him, even though he didn't move an inch.

✲ ✲ ✲

The afternoon sun came out to supply some warmth to the chilly day. They had walked for miles. At least that's what it felt like to Star. "How much further do we have to go?"

"What, are you tired?"

"No, I'm just curious. It seems like we've been walking forever. I thought your dad said that this place was nearby?"

"It was, but we've moved since then. At this pace we have at least another three or four hours before we get there. Do you want to stop?"

"No, we can keep going." She paused. "Can I ask you something?"

"Sure," Jacy replied as he helped her over a log.

"Where are we?"

Jacy didn't answer. Star stopped, so he turned to see her expression. "I said you can ask a question, but I didn't say I was going to answer," he laughed and pulled her along.

"Oh, come on. After we have the dagger, how are we supposed to use it if he doesn't know where we are?"

"Trust me, he knows that you're with us. Sooner or later he'll come for you."

"If he knows where we are, then why hasn't he come for me?"

"Several decades ago, the elders thought that it would be best if a portion of the tribe separated to protect you, the last Starfire. Jerick had no idea where we were until…"

"Until what?"

"Look," Jacy turned around and said, "I've said too much already. The point is that the less you know, the better it is for both you and your mother. He may try and hurt her just to get to you. And the only reason why you know about the dagger is because you're the only one that can retrieve it. Jerick doesn't even know about it."

Star didn't realize how much of an impact she had on his whole family. She already had Jacy's happiness hanging over her head, and now she'd found out that they left their people to take care of her. "I'm sorry, I didn't know. I guess they left that part out of the story."

"It's not a story, Princess," Jacy said, grabbing her hand to make her stop and look at him. "It's your life. You need to face the fact that this is all about you, all of it. We probably wouldn't even still exist if it wasn't for Lucero and the gift that he gave us years ago. Yes, my people have had to deal with a lot, but it has all come down to this moment. You have to promise me that you won't let us down, that you won't let me down, or this will all have been for nothing."

Star hated attention, and she hated people fussing over her. Her grandparents used to beg for her to come over all the time, but her mom would say no. She remembered them fussing over her as she cried to go with her Nana, but the answer was always no. Only after her father died did she finally get the opportunity to visit. Even then the reason for the visit was to keep her isolated and detached from world. She wanted to run away and forget that any of this was happening. She had gotten Jacy mad at her again, and not only had lives been ruined because of her, but the world's fate was in her hands.

"Star, come back to me," Jacy yelled. When he realized that he had broken her invisible barrier, he asked, "Where did you go just now?"

"Please don't. I...I can't take this anymore." Tears began to stream down Star's face. "This is too much. How could they think that a seventeen-year-old could live like this? That you and your people could live like this?" Her body began to shake, and a spark gleamed in the irises of her eyes.

"Star," Jacy said, pulling her into his arms. "I'm sorry. I just had to make you understand. I..." He stopped before he let the words leave his mouth. His father knew what he was about to say and made him stop. "Look at me. We're in this together, okay? You, me, and the pack."

Star wiped her face and began to walk with Jacy. He put his fist to his mouth like a microphone. "So, Princess, when this is over, where do you plan on spending eternity?"

Star composed herself and responded by saying, "I'm going to Disney World!"

✫ ✫ ✫

An hour passed, and Star was getting hungry, so they stopped to eat lunch. The day had grown colder, and Star's jacket wasn't as comforting as it had been six hours ago.

Jacy sat next to her on a large stone that barely fit the two of them, but he noticed that the chattering coming from Star's mouth wasn't because she was chewing. He wrapped his arms around her to help her get warmed up and then pulled out a sandwich for himself.

"Have you ever wondered why you're able to live long but not forever?"

"Not until recently. Growing old is the natural way of life, so we just have to play with what we we're dealt, even when we're given a wild card." Star gave him a look, and Jacy laughed. "There's a story about one of the older Night Howlers. It wasn't a time where our services were needed, so he grew restless and started to spend his time running around recklessly. They called him Evel Knievel Ted. He was the daredevil around the reservation, always trying to defy the law of physics. One day he did one too many tricks on his bike and impaled himself on a tree. He had already crushed his skull, broken bones, and even lost a finger in the past, but it was a branch that went straight through his heart that killed him."

"So what made you think about it recently?"

Jacy couldn't tell her his true feelings. However, he could tell her what he wanted to do after the whole ordeal was over. Maybe it would also change the subject. He breathed deeply and said, "I've never really gotten away before. I want to get a truck and travel around the country. You know, one big road trip." Jacy smiled as he packed away the trash from their lunch into his backpack. "You want to come? I'm sure Stephen will let you ride shotgun."

"Sure, why not? I actually had the same idea, except I wanted to travel around the world. Unfortunately, my mom says that I have to finish college first. Hey, maybe after all of this, I can tell her I have an eternity to finish and she'll let me wait until after our trip." She smiled and stood up.

"Hey, you will be eighteen, after all. It'll be your choice!" He looked at the path ahead, saying, "Let's get going. We're almost there."

They walked for another half an hour and came to a cliff that looked out to a body of water. The view was amazing, but that was only until Jacy said, "It's down there."

Star's eyes widened, but she knew that the task had to be done. They walked over to two trees that were joined by overgrown brush.

Jacy moved them aside, pulling some up from the earth. Clearing them revealed a trail that led down to a path that wrapped along the cliff.

"You might want to take off your gloves so that you can hold on to the vines," Jacy said, still clearing shrubs along the way.

Star peered down at the water while she stuffed her mittens in her pocket.

"You're not afraid, are you?"

"No, I'm okay."

"Good, because the rest of the trail is very small and rocky," Jacy said, pulling her closer to the rocky wall.

It was rocky, just like Jacy had mentioned, but the vines were very helpful. Jacy moved along the wall with ease. It amazed Star how he was able to maneuver around the obstacles along the trail with his large body. It wasn't long before they reached the opening that was covered with overgrown shrubs, just like the main entrance to the path. Jacy pulled them down and took out a flashlight.

He looked over at Star and said, "Here we go."

Their lights flickered against the muddy walls that were also riddled with vines. Jacy led the way through the opening as Star walked slowly behind.

"When was the last time you were here?" she asked.

"Um, about twelve years ago. Some kids get sweet sixteen parties or Bar Mitzvahs. I got a cave," he laughed.

Star followed, stumbling on the rocks below. The cave was massive compared to the trail that led to it. There were two more openings that appeared in front of them.

"It's this way." Jacy motioned to the entrance on the right.

Star heard the hissing of a possible snake that lurked nearby and grabbed Jacy's hand. Jacy laughed and pulled her deeper into the cave, going downward. Star couldn't hold back her fear of the space and grabbed on to Jacy's arm, as his hand just wasn't enough.

"It's okay. It's not too much further."

They continued walking until they came to a room with paintings on the wall. Star recognized Felix's bright red hair. Even though the drawings had aged, his presence still made its mark. The Night Howlers were also in the paintings. They were large, in wolf and human form, but, Star thought, the paintings on the wall told only half the story. It was the story of what was waiting for her inside, but they didn't show what she would have to face afterward. Jacy pulled her along through a tiny opening that led to a roped bridge. He put down his bag and handed her the flashlight. He reached into the side of the bag, took out a lighter, and lit a stick that hung on the wall as Star stood staring at the bridge that they would most likely need to cross in order to get to the dagger.

"Please don't tell me."

"Yes, we have to. Look, I'll even go first to show you that it's fine." Jacy smiled at Star and began to walk across. He walked about half of the way and then brought up his hand, motioning Star to join him.

Star followed slowly, stepping over the planks of wood that had rotted away. Jacy made it to the other side while Star still looked at the gaping black hole below.

"Come on, Star. At this rate, we won't be home until tomorrow morning," Jacy laughed.

Just then the rope began to unravel, releasing it from the side they had just left. Star lost her grip on the flashlight, and it circled out of sight, illuminating the endless hole below. She began to run to Jacy as the rope continued to unravel. Star leaped as the bridge crumbled away and caught the edge of a rock that stuck out from the hole. Jacy caught her hand just as she started to slip and pulled her up. Her heart raced as Jacy held on to her so tightly that her ribs ached in pain. Jacy realized how tight he was holding on and let her go.

"I'm sorry."

Star bent over and grabbed her side. "It's okay. Ow!," she cried out, looking at her wrist that had begun to bleed.

Jacy looked at her injured wrist and pulled it to his mouth. He wiped away the blood with his thumb and licked the open wound. "Look, all better," he said and kissed it.

Star was grossed out until she noticed that the bleeding had stopped. "How did you do that?"

"I think the better question is why does your blood tingle like Pop Rocks?" Jacy laughed and walked over to the wall lighting the torch that hung from it.

"What's going on? Did we hit a dead end?"

"No, I just have to find the opening. There's sediment covering it." Jacy ran his hand along the wall until he stopped and began to brush dirt away. There lay the crystal-like star Jacy's dad had mentioned.

"How are we going to get in?"

Jacy turned to her and smiled. "I'd cover my face if I were you."

Star stepped away and covered her face. Jacy pulled his fist back and landed a punch directly in the center of the star. A portion of the wall came tumbling down as a bright light beamed from the glass room, blinding Jacy. Star pulled her hands from her face and was instantly drawn to the light. Jacy held her arm while he escorted her over the rocks that had fallen from his invasion while still trying to block out the light from his eyes. Inside Star could see stars holding the dagger in place with their brilliant glow.

"Can you hear that?" Star whispered. "It's calling out to me."

Jacy stood silent, trying to hear the voices, as Star walked ahead into the ring of stars that circled the floor. Even with his accelerated hearing, he couldn't hear it.

She stepped closer and closer, until she was completely in the circle. A bright light encased her and blew Jacy against the wall, bringing the rest of it down with him. Star stood with her eyes wide open, affixed on the stars that called out to her, unaware of what had happened to Jacy. Star reached out with both hands to retrieve the dagger. The stars that held it circled around her and shot into the sides of her skull. The dagger fell from her hands, and she also fell, joining it on the ground.

The area dimmed, and all that remained was the flickering blaze from the stick that Jacy had lit. He collected himself and looked into the room to find Star unconscious and the dagger lying beside her. Jacy ran over to her and tried to wake her, but she wouldn't open her eyes.

Jacy pulled Star into his arms and picked up the dagger. He walked to the cliff, trying to figure out how he would get across. He threw her over his shoulder and held the dagger in his hand along with Star's legs. He walked a few steps backward and then hurled their bodies across the pit below, landing just as sure as if he had jumped only five feet. He walked over to his backpack and put the dagger inside. Then he pulled Star from his shoulder to replace her with the bag. He carried her in his arms, using his wolf-assisted eyes to make his way out of the cave.

October 7

Star's eyes began to wave beneath her eyelids. "She's waking up!" Jacy yelled out as Star's eye's opened. He was shocked at their appearance. Star looked back, but didn't say anything.

Ruth, Kaya, and Jessie ran into the room. They all gazed at Star's new eyes that sparkled like diamonds.

"Are you okay?" Ruth called out as she walked over with a glass of water. "Are you thirsty?" She put the glass up to Star's mouth and lifted her head to drink without an answer. Star only drank half and pulled away.

"How long have I been like this?" she asked with a cracking voice.

Kaya sat on the bed, stroking her leg, and replied, "Almost four days."

Jessie unfolded his arms and motioned for them all to leave. "Let's give them some space to talk."

They exited the room as Jacy sat down beside Star on the bed. "I don't know what happened. There was a bright light that blew me away, and when I got up, you were out."

"I was with Lucero," Star replied. "He was explaining what happened to me." Star brought her hand over weakly to see if she still possessed her bracelet.

Jacy noticed and reassured her it was still there.

"Home, it's a piece of home."

"I think you need to rest."

"No, he told me that he gave it as a gift, a piece of home that I can always carry with me. He called me Jaelyn." She stroked the bracelet in her hand, saying, "He said that my life will be filled with a power beyond my imagination, but I could never return to him. He said that the stars are all that will link us, but now that he's given me even more power before I've developed on my own, it can kill my human life before I reach my eighteenth birthday. He said that Jerick must be killed before I perish."

Jacy's face flushed with her tale, while her body still lay weak, embracing the new being that lay awake inside her.

The Happening

November 27

Even though Star stayed up with Ruth and Kaya to help prepare for Thanksgiving Day, she still wasn't looking forward to it. She called her mother the minute she woke up. It was just as hard for her not having Star with her as it was for Star. She assured her that she was okay, even though she seemed to be losing her appetite. Her bracelet hung on her wrist like an ornament dangling from a Christmas tree, and she grew weak, but she chose to spare her mother from concern. She was happy to hear that she hadn't had any recent episodes of walking in her sleep, but Star knew that she needed them if she was going to survive. She couldn't, however, tell her about that or that her days would come to an end soon as well. She choked out a good-bye at the end of her call, not knowing if that would be the last time she would ever be able to say it.

Ruth must have known it was going to be hard for Star to handle as well. Before she headed down to start preparing for the day's festivities, she came in to help Star with her hair and to talk. She made a braid across the top of her hair to hold the rest back in soft curls. Star enjoyed their talks. They were just like the ones she used to have with her mom. She really needed it to get through the rest of today.

✻ ✻ ✻

The day wasn't turning out so bad. It was just like the party that was thrown for her when she came. Everyone was there. There were so many people in the house that those who weren't affected by the cold took solace from the crowded area outside. The girls took care of the food with their moms, and this time Cadee was even there to help out. Star noticed her looking at her curiously, but she didn't say anything until she couldn't take it anymore.

"Is there something wrong, Cadee?" Star asked with an awkward smile. The words felt somewhat confrontational to her, but she hated being watched.

"Oh, no, there's nothing wrong," she giggled and pursed her lips. "I just noticed that, uh…"

Star looked, waiting for her response.

"Well, uh, have you lost weight, Star?"

Kaya gave her a nudge.

"Hey, what did I say?"

"Nothing, just keep chopping."

Star didn't pay her any mind. She was strong-minded, just like Kaya. That's probably why they got along so well. There seemed to be someone for everyone here, as a friend or companion. They had each other; Jacy had Stephen; Cody had Poe; Chenoa had Myra. She enjoyed each of them, but kind of felt left out. She figured because she wasn't going to be there long, she could probably just borrow a little from each of them.

After the food was all prepared, everyone gathered around the kitchen area or poked their heads in to hear Jessie speak.

"I am very happy to have all of you with us today. This is a very special time for our people. Not only a time to give thanks, but to also appreciate the gift and duties we have been given. We have been given a great responsibility and have completed one of our tasks. The greatest is yet to come. We don't know when this may happen, but what we do know is that this is our purpose. We are very thankful this year to have you with us, Starfire. It is our honor to have you with us. Through my father's memories, I have known your great-grandmother. She would've been proud of you. The sacrifice you may have to make and that she was unable to achieve will not be for naught. The Rockne people are honored to protect and be with you on your journey. According to legends, this may be our last Thanksgiving together, but we now have the opportunity to change the story. We must make today and every day hereafter a day of thanksgiving, for our people have also made sacrifices, but those sacrifices have not gone unnoticed. Our reward is yet to come. Now, I say to you all, fellowship and give your love. Eat and give thanks."

They all began to cheer and hug one another, telling everyone that they were thankful to have them and that they loved them. Star was swallowed by the arms of her cousins and the rest of the Rockne people.

Jessie came to hug her and said, "I meant every word, Starfire. We're thankful for having you and will help you to succeed in your mission. We are in this together, kiddo."

Star smiled and took in a deep breath after he let go.

Jessie smiled. "Sorry, I forget my own strength sometimes."

Jacy came up behind him and opened his arms to embrace her. She obliged and caved in to them. He kissed her on the cheek and said, "Love you."

"Love you too," Star replied playfully and pulled away. The look in Jacy's eyes confused her. But she didn't have time to react.

Jessie tapped Jacy on the shoulder and said, "Let's let her get something to eat."

Jacy set her down as everyone began to make their way to the tables to fix their food. It was all set up buffet style. They had brought in a folding table and set it up alongside the dining room table. Star couldn't wait to tell her mom about it.

Leakesh was in line behind Star and insisted on placing a spoonful of potatoes on her plate. "Men like women with meat on their bones," she laughed and hip-bumped Star. She was definitely Cadee's mom.

Later that evening, Cody was able to tell her what had happened with their great-grandfather. That it took him time to get over Beth, but he was able to move on. He had just passed away two years ago from old age. He said that he'd really loved Beth, but her parents just wouldn't let her stay after they found out they were together. Times were different then. Her being with him just wasn't cool. They didn't find out she was pregnant until after she left. But it was too late, and her grandmother was given away, or so they were told. Star knew that it was true. She told him that her grandmother had been raised by her aunt. She was able to visit her mother, but she was out of it most of the time and passed away fairly young, so Beth never really got to know her, something that Star now realized happened quite often in her family and the reason why.

They stayed over late, and Star fought to stay awake. She hated being tired all the time. She had been having so much fun with the pack that she'd hardly hung out with Kaya and Cadee at all. They ripped on each other like brothers. They were brothers. Even though they were born from different parents, they shared a bond that couldn't be broken.

November 28

Star was lying on her bed sketching when Kaya burst in the door saying, "It's time to begin Christmas shopping! I love this time of year." She was holding her laptop in one hand and an apple in the other.

"Shopping online for Christmas presents isn't as fun as going to the store," replied Star as she slunk her cheek into her hand.

"Think fast!" Kaya threw the apple over to Star with a smile. She barely caught it before Kaya sat down. "Mom told me to bring you something to snack on. And don't ruin it for me. Shopping can be fun no matter how you do it."

"Sorry," Star said, sitting up. She took a bite out of the apple and looked over at Kaya's computer.

"So I'll just order what Chenoa and I want from you. What do you want to get Jacy?"

"I don't know."

"Well here's a pen and paper. Write down what you want to get him, and I'll order it.

Star sat staring at the blank piece of paper with her new eyes. She still hadn't gotten used to them. They were like flashlights in the dark, sparkling in the darkened sky. Her vision was clear and seemed to peer out further than her human vision. They still scared her whenever she caught a glimpse of them in the mirror. She guessed that they were her father's eyes. She couldn't see him when he spoke, but she heard his voice. His stern and powerful voice commanded her attention. She would've gone to the cave sooner if he'd demanded her to. She still couldn't believe that the cave was just as Jessie described it, and its treasures were still to be explored. She felt tired more often now, but she didn't feel as though she possessed the power that Lucero told her awaited her. She thought back to her time in the woods with Jacy. She couldn't believe that he also wanted to travel just as she did. The thought made her want to live and fulfill her destiny even more.

That's it! Star thought to herself and scribbled her answer down on the paper.

December 13

There had been a great snowfall the night before, as Mother Nature didn't care what day the calendar reserved for the first day of winter. Star slept in late, but Chenoa couldn't help herself with all of the snow lingering outside the window, waiting to be played in. Jacy was able to hold her at bay for a little while, but after she ate breakfast and Star still wasn't downstairs, she made her way up to her room.

Star felt Chenoa's presence when she lay down next to her. She opened her eyes and smiled at the little girl. "Good morning, Tweety." She had picked it up from Jacy because of her yellow complexion and little pink nose. "Please, just five more minutes," Star pleaded as she turned over.

"The snow will melt by then."

"Oh, I'm pretty sure that won't happen," Jacy laughed as he stood by the door. "I'm sorry, she got away from me."

"Some protector you turned out to be," Star laughed and sat up. "Okay, give me some time to take a shower and get dressed, okay?" She smiled at Chenoa.

"Okay, I'll be waiting," she replied and rolled off the bed.

✲ ✲ ✲

Star took her shower and put on some clothes to enjoy the winter wonderland that awaited her presence outside. Ruth was heading to the living room when Star came downstairs. She motioned with her head, pointing to the table saying, "I left some breakfast on the table for you."

"Thank you," Star replied and headed for the door.

"You're not going to eat before you go out?"

"No, I can eat later. Thank you for thinking of me."

"It was my pleasure." She smiled. "Jacy and Chenoa already got a head start."

"Look, it's Star!" Jacy called out, and Chenoa threw snow at him as Star walked out the door. He wore only a T-shirt and cargo shorts with boots.

"Anyone that didn't know you would think you were crazy for wearing that," Star laughed, pointing at his shorts.

"Well, it's easier to deal with than wet jeans. Come and help us make a snowman."

☆ ☆ ☆

The lawn was riddled with snow angels that surrounded the less than perfect snowman. His carrot nose went perfectly with his button eyes and twiggy arms. Star's fingertips had turned as red as Chenoa's nose, and her scarf was soaking wet, but she continued lifting it to block Jacy's snowballs. He had found some way to manage the speed on his balls, because the first two or three had surely left a bruise on Star's legs and shoulder. Star bent down to collect snow in retaliation while Jacy picked up Chenoa to use her as a shield. She began to form the cold snow into a ball as a spark shot through her glove and melted the snow into water. A spark of light lingered for a split second and disappeared. They all stood amazed. Their eyes gazed at the hole that now bared the palm of Star's hand.

"How did you do that?" Jacy asked while he still held Chenoa's body, dangling beneath him.

"I...I don't know."

Jacy put Chenoa down and told her to go inside.

"Aw, but I don't want to, Uncle Jace." Chenoa looked up and crossed her arms.

"Now, Chenoa Jackson," Jacy ordered the girl, pointing to the door without removing his eyes from what had just beamed from Star's hand. Chenoa knew she'd better go inside this time, because he'd used her full name.

He walked over to Star and pulled off the ruined mitten. Her hand told no tale of what had just happened. He turned it over in his hands and looked at Star. "How was that possible? It was like a star burst from the palm of your hand, but there's nothing. Your hand is perfectly fine."

They both looked up when Jessie opened the back door and came outside. "So you're getting your powers."

"I guess, but I don't know how it happened."

"Too bad they couldn't have come with an instruction manual," Jacy laughed. "Sorry." He shrugged. "Well, what were you thinking about before it happened?"

"I was just thinking about hitting you," Star replied.

"It has to be something else," Jessie responded, running his fingers through his hair. "How about thinking about what you were feeling during that time?"

"What I was feeling?" Star smiled.

"Come on, it can't hurt," said Jacy.

Star closed her eyes and tried to conjure up what she had been feeling at that moment. Suddenly a surge of energy awoke inside her. It felt like some hot and tingly liquid building up inside her, slowly making her lift her hand. She turned it over, disintegrating the mitten that still remained on her hand, and one by one she opened her fingers to reveal a single star that hung in the open sky over her palm. She opened her eyes as she realized what she had created. She lifted her hand as Jacy and his father took a step back. Their eyes were bright and filled with the light that hovered over her outstretched hand. Star touched the star with her other hand. With each touch it made tiny little sparking noises. Star laughed because it made her fingers tingle. The star slowly faded and was gone.

Jessie and Jacy stood still, looking at what Star had just done. "You truly are Starfire," Jessie crooned and walked over to her. He took her face in his large hand and lifted it up to him. "This is only the beginning."

December 24

Kaya managed to find ways that Chenoa could keep Jacy busy while Star made the final touches to his Christmas gift. She wrapped the box with blue wrapping paper that was riddled with silver snowflakes that twinkled and tied a big blue bow around it like her mother used to do. She would always wrap the best gift with a large bow under the tree. Thanksgiving was hard without her, but Christmas was becoming even harder. Her mother had to console her over the phone when she could no longer hold back her tears. She told her that this was for the best and that none of the gifts she was ever given could compare to giving birth to her.

Star went downstairs to join everyone sitting in the living room. The Christmas tree that sat in the corner lit the room. Gifts skirted the tree, all but for one. Star didn't want to bring it down while Jacy was sitting there. They made room for her on the couch so that she could join them while they watched *A Christmas Story*. After the movie was over, Jessie and Ruth headed upstairs with Chenoa while the rest stayed downstairs watching movies. Childhood anxiety still lingered, but no one would say it. Jacy had gone to sit on the floor so he could search for another movie to watch.

"So, Kaya, what did I get you and Chenoa for Christmas?"

"I don't know, but if you want me to open my gift, I can." She smiled, heading toward the tree.

"Oh, whatever, Kaya," laughed Star. "I guess we'll have to wait and see it tomorrow."

"So what did you get me?" Jacy looked up and questioned Star.

"You'll have to wait for tomorrow too." Star smiled and patted his head. She lay down and clutched the couch pillow, fighting yet again to stay awake.

The movie had just begun when Kaya decided to call it a night since she couldn't open any gifts and her mom had threatened to cut off their hands if they touched the food for tomorrow. Star decided to just stay up with Jacy and continue watching movies.

That was until he turned and said, "She should've held out. It's Christmas!" He popped up and went over to the tree. He ruffled behind the gifts until he found a small box. He walked over, sat down in front of Star, and said, "Merry Christmas, Princess."

He held up the red box to her as she sat up, curious. "Won't we get into trouble?"

"No, don't worry about my mom. Her bark is worse than her bite."

Star smiled and said, "Wait right here then." She ran up the stairs and grabbed his gift from underneath the bed, where she had hidden it. She tiptoed back downstairs and sat on the couch next to Jacy. She turned and faced him, holding out her gift. "You go first."

He handed her the box, and he took hers. He pulled at the blue ribbon, tore off the wrapping paper, and pulled the box open. Inside he found an atlas.

Star smiled as he pulled it out of the box. "It's not much, but I've had to live in several different places and have been to a couple of cool places, so I marked some of the ones I thought you guys might like. I figured we would have enough time to figure out where else you'd want to visit."

"Wow, when I heard you guys talking about gifts, I never would've thought this was what you came up with. I thought I was going to get a shirt or something."

"Do you like it?"

"I love it!" he said as he flipped through the pages to find the cities she'd once lived in.

"Wait a second," Star said, putting her hand on the book that was between them. "How did you know?"

Jacy smiled. "Felix told us every time you moved. You know, just in case you needed us." He shrugged. "Now," he said as he lifted her box from the couch, "open your gift."

Star took it from him and smiled as she ripped off the shimmering green bow and placed it to the side. She tore off the wrapping paper and opened the box, smiling at Jacy. She pulled back the lid and saw a ring. Star smiled, but was also puzzled.

Jacy saw the look on her face and pulled out the ring. "I saw it and thought of you." It was a thin band with tiny diamonds going halfway around it. "The stones reminded me of your eyes, and I thought you would like it. It's a stupid gift."

"No, I love it." Star smiled as she grabbed for it.

Jacy turned and said, "No, I'll take it back."

"Please, I want it. I really like it. I was just a little shocked. I thought it was a pair of earrings or something."

Jacy turned back around to look at Star and said with a wishful grin, "I'll give it back if you promise to wear it all the time."

"Promise. Cross my heart and hope to die," Star replied, drawing an X over her heart. Star grabbed for the ring again, but Jacy pulled it away.

"Here, let me." Jacy took her right hand in his and placed the ring on her ring finger. His fingers lingered on hers, and then he let her hand go. "I hope that you won't ever die." He looked up at her and said, "It's a perfect fit."

"Yeah, and it matches my bracelet." Star smiled and held out her hand. "Thank you," she said, kissing him on his cheek and hugging his neck.

Jacy held on a little longer than he should've and tried to play it off. "How about we mark some of the other places we want to go?" Jacy went into the kitchen and came back with a notebook and two pens. He handed one of them, along with the notebook, to Star. "I'll navigate while you write, deal?"

"Deal."

The movie played out while Star lay back on the couch to get cozy. Jacy called out areas that he recognized and had always wanted to go so that she could write them down. He was on his fourteenth destination when he heard her pen drop. Jacy looked over and saw that Star had dozed off. He laughed and turned off the TV. He closed his book, collected the remnants of the wrapping paper and the notebook Star had been writing in. On the corner of the page, he saw a small picture she had drawn of him smiling. *She was such an amazing artist, but she never shared it with anyone,* he thought to himself. He turned off the lights on the tree and carried Star upstairs to bed.

Star woke up still in her clothes from the night before. Jacy stood in front of her with his hands in his pockets, saying, "Good morning. Everyone's downstairs waiting for you."

She wiped her face and sat up a little woozy.

"Are you okay?"

"Um, yeah, let me go and brush my teeth, and I'll be down."

Jacy walked to the door. "Merry Christmas, Princess."

Star smiled. "Merry Christmas."

"Well, when did you go to bed?" Kaya said to Star as she walked into the living room.

"I'm sorry," Star apologized for her appearance while she tugged on her T-shirt.

"Merry Christmas, sweetie," Ruth called out to her. Jessie smiled and lifted his coffee mug up to her, gesturing the same.

Jessie and Ruth sat on the couch while everyone tore through their gifts. Jacy got the clothes that he was dreading. He hoped that he would finally get a car, but not this year. His mom always did the Christmas and birthday shopping for the family so that he and his father wouldn't know what everyone was getting. Star realized that Kaya must have gotten that from her mom after trying to shop for Jacy. Even with them writing down what she had finally decided to get him, he still knew that they were shopping. Luckily Kaya got him the watch that he wanted so he wasn't completely disappointed, and for Star she got a sweater dress and high-heeled boots.

"I've never worn heels before, Kaya."

"There's a first time for everything, and besides, I'll teach you. You can wear it today."

"Great, I can't wait," she replied sarcastically.

The Long Feathers got Star a necklace with a star pendant to match her bracelet, and a pair of earrings. Star got Kaya a purse that she said she'd had her eye on for months, and for Chenoa, a bicycle.

"Great gifts, huh, Star?"

Star laughed, "Yeah, I'm glad you liked them."

"Hey, where's your gift for Jacy?"

"I gave it to him last night."

Jacy sat against the recliner and smiled.

"Hey, I thought you guys were supposed to wait until today?"

"It was as of twelve a.m., Kay," Jacy replied and rolled his eyes.

"So let me see."

"See what? Oh," Star said when she understood what Kaya was saying. Star held out her hand and showed her the ring.

A crease formed in Kaya's brow and said, "Aren't you wearing it on the wrong hand?"

"What?"

"Kaya," Jessie said in a stern voice.

"I'm sorry," Kaya responded, fumbling her words. "I was thinking from this angle that you had it on your left hand. It's bad luck to wear any ring but the wedding ring on that finger."

Star pulled her hand back and said, "I know. You can be a weirdo sometimes, you know."

✫ ✫ ✫

Star helped Jacy and Chenoa clean up the trash, and Jessie headed to the kitchen to raid the fridge. Star finally noticed that everyone was already dressed.

What time is it anyway? she thought to herself. She looked at the clock on the microwave to read 12:47. She didn't realize she had slept so long.

"Go and take your shower so that we can start your lessons. Everyone's going to start coming over around three, so we want to have you looking great before then."

Star obliged and went upstairs with her gifts. After he was sure that Star was in the shower, Jacy turned to scream at Kaya, "What were you thinking?"

"I'm sorry, Jace. I thought that you told her. It was my mistake. When I saw the ring, I just assumed."

"Jacy knows his responsibilities and that his feelings may compromise the situation. He'll be able to tell her in due time, but until then, no more from you two. At least not in front of her," Jessie ordered and went back into the living room to eat.

"How do you even know she would accept? Did she say something to you?"

"Ah, so you want to know if we talk about you when you're not around? Relax. Dad would've heard it if you didn't. I will say this. You are the only person she allows to call her Princess."

"Oh, I never noticed." Jacy smiled and blushed beneath his warm skin.

✫ ✫ ✫

Star popped off the tag to her new dress and pulled it over her head. It was a lavender knit dress that came in at her waist and flowed out about four inches above her knee. The collar plunged down from her neck into a V shape, but didn't show too much cleavage. It fit perfectly, along with the ring that adorned her finger. Star beamed looking down at the ring. It probably held some meaning other than it just being a gift he found in the store, but she didn't want to read too much into it. Jacy could've just bought the ring for the reasons he mentioned, nothing more. He never said he liked her, and they fought every other week over the smallest things. Well, at least they did before she claimed the dagger. It sat on her dresser, wrapped in a cloth of velvet. It was the one thing on Earth that could kill Jerick, but it just sat there collecting dust while they waited for his arrival. Star pushed it aside and pulled out her comb and brush. She parted her hair in the center and brushed it into place. Then she put on the necklace and earrings the Long Feathers had given her and stared at the boots lying in the box. Her bare feet cringed at the sight of them. They were brown and had a heel that was at least four inches high. Star tugged at her fitted sleeves until she heard a knock at the door.

"It's me," Kaya called out and entered the room. "Are you ready for your lesson?"

"Not as much as you are," Star laughed as she plopped on the bed and pulled on her socks.

"It's simple. Just slip them on and walk around. You'll see."

Star pulled on the boots and stood up. They fit to her legs like a glove. She walked over to the door and then back to the bed.

"That's it. You're a natural." Kaya smiled and lay down on the bed. "Don't be shocked if they're missing now and again, though. They're really cute! I might need to borrow them from time to time."

"They are starting to grow on me." Star smiled, peering down at her first heels.

"Can I ask you something?"

"Sure," Star replied, abandoning the gaze from her boots.

"Why is it that you only allow Jacy to call you Princess?"

"What? I don't do that, do I?" she questioned as she slumped back on the bed.

"Yeah, you do. You like him, don't you?"

Star turned and looked at Kaya, but didn't answer.

✲ ✲ ✲

The night was filled with more gifts and laughter. Jacy got more clothes, but was even happier to get money to put toward his truck. Kaya and Star received clothes as well, while Chenoa raked in more toys. She was definitely occupied for the day. Star was happy because she wasn't really in the mood to play out in the snow today, especially not in heels. Jacy hung out on the porch with the other guys, and Star joined the girls in the kitchen to help cook. She was learning a lot from them. Sometimes she would just hang around when her mother would cook. She would watch her dance around the kitchen and lend a hand when she was needed. Her new family changed the menu so often and had so many people to feed that Star couldn't help but to lend a hand.

Outside, the elders and the pack gathered. They had grown curious about Jerick's return because he still hadn't come back.

"You'll need to ask her about her dreams," Ben said to Jacy before he took a sip of his coffee.

"She doesn't like to talk about them, but I'll see what I can get out of her," Jacy responded.

"I know this has been difficult for you, but you have been doing a great job." Jack looked at Jacy and then to the rest. "All of you have."

Jessie nodded and said, "He's never stayed away this long. When he came for Beth, he tried two or three times a month. Something's not right. We have to stay focused on this one. He won't be hard to kill, but his death is needed to help Starfire survive. I can tell she's growing weaker by the minute. She sleeps longer and barely ever eats. The being inside her is taking over and will soon take her away."

"We must not allow that to happen!" Jacy yelled and shot up with a low growl leaving his throat.

The women heard him in the kitchen, but diverted Star away from the door.

"Calm down, son," Grandpa Joe said, now standing beside Jacy. "I think it's time we tell her where she is. We will let him into our home and dispatch him where he stands." He turned and looked at them all. "This is our final chance to do things right. We will not fail."

☆ ☆ ☆

After dinner, everyone went home, which shocked Star because normally at least the pack stayed behind and hung out with Jacy. Instead they started the dishes as usual. Star still wore her heels, and Jacy couldn't help but notice them.

"You're really getting a hang of those heels, aren't you?"

Star smiled. "Yeah, I can't wait for my mom to see me in them."

"I think that's the first time I've heard you talk about seeing her again, well, since…"

"Oh, yeah, I decided that I shouldn't think about the things I might miss out on. Instead I'll think about what I'm going to do."

Jacy finished up the dishes, and Star went to play with Chenoa. He wiped down the countertop, wishing that he could wipe away what was happening. Grandpa Joe's ruling lay on his mind like a ton of bricks. It was so hard being in everyone's mind all the time. All they had to do was tunnel in, and their voice rang as clear as if you were standing right in front of them. It was harder for him because his father was Alpha. Though his grandfather stood aside to allow Jessie control the pack, his opinions and callings still meant a lot to them. Jacy decided that though he was told to tell Star where she was, he felt it best to still keep her in the dark. Feeling secure about his decision, he knew that it was pure selfishness on his behalf. Jerick was going to come sooner or later, but he would rather it be later. Though they were warned that the power may kill her before her birthday, she didn't appear to be slowing down that much.

"*Dude, just admit that you don't want her to know where she is, because if she does, Jerick will come, we'll kill him, and then she will be free to live her life,*" Cody blurted out before he felt Jacy making him shut up.

He didn't want to admit it, but what Cody was saying was true. He looked at her as she began to pirouette in the dining room with Chenoa. He pushed for her to want to live, but he was selfishly asking her to live for him. His whole existence seemed to be based on protecting her. What would he do without her? Traveling around the country with the guys was going to be amazing, but she was now a part of that dream. He couldn't imagine doing it without her.

"*This will be your burden to bear if you take this route, son,*" Jessie said with his inner voice from around the corner, where he still sat in the living room with Ruth. "*I have faith in you to make the right decision.*"

✵ ✵ ✵

It had become common for Star and Jacy to stay up later than everyone else, but tonight had taken its toll on Star. She said goodnight to everyone and went upstairs. She kicked off the boots that she had just begun to love, but after cleaning the kitchen and dancing around with Chenoa, they weren't her favorite. She grabbed her fleece pajamas that were covered in ice cream cones out of the closet and went to take a shower. She removed her new dress and undergarments, placing them on the shelf. She then stepped into the shower and let the water stream down her back as she leaned for support on the wall. She felt dizzy, but caught herself before she fell down. Her legs still felt a little wobbly, so she slid down the side wall of the shower and let the water continue to pour down on her.

When she came back to the room, Jacy was already there, laying out his bed, a quilt his mom had made and a fleece blanket.

"I thought you were going to hang out with the guys?"

"Not tonight, I figured I'd get some sleep since I didn't really get any last night. Some of us were planning our future while the other was supposed to be dictating," Jacy replied with a crooked smile.

"Well, some of us need to sleep. We can't all stay up howling at the moon."

Jacy laughed and charged at her like he was going to attack, but only grabbed her in a bear hug and rustled her hair. "Good one!"

Star had lain down and begun to let the night take her away when she heard Jacy's voice.

"Star, I need to ask you something."

Star sat up to see what Jacy wanted. He crawled up to the end of his former bed and swallowed deeply. He knew that his question may upset her, but he had to do what he was told. He hung his head and then looked at Star, regretting every word that was about to leave his mouth. "Have you dreamt of him, of Jerick, lately?"

Star paused, but she knew that an answer was needed. "No, I haven't. Not since the night on the roof," she replied as she tried to hide her face by brushing away some of her hair. Star remembered their last encounter and the sound of his voice. He'd sounded scared and hurt. All he had said was that they'd hurt him. Did he mean the pack? Was he here but they hadn't told her? She shook off the thought knowing one day he would have to be killed in order for her to live. But why did it feel so bad?

"Where were you just now?"

"I was just thinking about something he said to me," she responded, but she wasn't sure why she had.

"What was it?" Jacy asked as he slid onto the bed, causing it to creak. Star motioned for him to be quiet because the bed squealed with the added weight. "It's okay. My dad would know if we were making out." Jacy smiled.

Star could feel her face flush over in embarrassment. She shook her head and replied, "I didn't mean that. I was saying be quiet so that we didn't wake anyone up."

"Well, yeah, who's ever been able to make out quietly?"

Star was shocked at how open he was. He never talked about that kind of stuff with her.

"There you go again."

"What?"

"Getting lost in your thoughts. You seem to get lost in your thoughts a lot lately."

"Oh, I hadn't noticed."

"Why don't you let anyone in? I mean, you've been here for months, and you still haven't let me in."

Star couldn't understand where this was all coming from. She had been a completely different person around them. Normally she would've still spent her days locked away in her room reading or drawing, not talking to anyone. Star lifted her hand and formed a star from her palm so that they could see one another clearly.

"What are you talking about? You've known more about me than I did," she whispered, but somehow it still held her anger.

"You only give me diluted versions of your dreams, and you've never shown me your drawings." It was Jacy that now displayed his anger in his whispers.

"My book, what do you know about my book?"

"I know that you are amazing. I…I mean your drawings are amazing, but you never express that side of you. You never let anyone in."

Star hung her head, now realizing that she was making her life just as sheltered as it had been when she was with her mother. She was setting hopes up for next year, but hadn't stopped to think about what she could be doing right now. The fun she could be having right now. The things she could be sharing right now.

Star smiled as she realized Jacy was staring at her, lost in one of her moments. "Hold on," she said and jumped off the bed. The star hung in its place.

Jacy sat in awe, watching the star shimmer without her assistance. "How did you do that? I mean, I've never seen you sustain it for so long and move without it."

"I've been practicing." Star smiled and held her book on her lap, sighing. "I don't really let anyone look in here. Not even my mother, so you better not laugh or tell anyone."

However, Star didn't know that he had already taken a peek, but he was able to mask it.

"I started this one two or three weeks before Felix came to visit. I know that I haven't shared my dreams with you, or anyone for that matter, but I just felt that they were private. When I came here, I barely remembered Jerick, but he began to visit me more often. The things that he said to me were like he was speaking to my soul. Looking back on it, I don't know if he was trying to help me get over the loss of my father and loneliness or if he was just saying those things to help himself in his plight. But the way he looked at me, it felt like being stuck in a trance. I never wanted to wake up."

Jacy put the book down and took her hand away from her face. Star hadn't realized that she had been crying. Jacy wrapped himself around her and leaned back against the headboard, laying her upon his chest, as she continued sobbing. The star lingered in the air as her breathing slowly calmed down. With Star's eyes sealed shut by her glittered tears, she fell asleep, and the star fizzled away.

December 26

Star awoke still nestled in his arms. Her hand that rested upon his stomach, moving with the rhythm of his breathing, began to slowly move across it. She slowly lifted her head with the sudden realization of last night's ending creeping into her mind. She was so embarrassed that she didn't even want to look at him. He finished lifting her head for her and smiled.

"Rough night, huh?"

Star nodded.

"Not a total bust, though, looks like there's something else we've learned about you."

Star slowly sat up as Jacy smiled. She looked at him with a puzzled look in her crystal-like eyes.

"You slept on my chest the whole night. Chenoa can't even tolerate me for ten minutes before she turns red."

Star reached out her hand and placed it on his arm.

"What do you feel?"

Star's blushed face turned to excitement when she felt Jacy's skin and it felt like the touch of a regular human. He still felt solid, like she was grabbing on to a heated rock, but he didn't feel like he was boiling hot.

Jacy laughed at the look on her face as well as the voices that chimed in his head.

Just then a knock was at the door, and Kaya walked in. Her eyes were focused on the two of them still lying in the bed. "Well, what's going on here? Mom told you to stay on the floor," she said, pointing at Jacy.

"Oh, stop it Kay, we weren't doing anything, not anymore anyway."

Star blushed. "We weren't doing anything at all. I just got upset about something, and Jacy..."

"You don't have to lie for my benefit, Star," Kaya laughed. "I have to go to work, and I wanted to borrow our new boots."

Jacy laughed. "I think she just got those for herself and used you as an excuse to buy them." She shot him a look and walked over to them, as they lay crumpled on the floor.

Star turned and got off the bed. "I'll make you a deal. "You can have them, but promise me that you'll let me borrow them from time to time."

"You have a deal!" Kaya threw her arm around her. "You're like the little sister I never wanted but I am definitely happy to have." She gave her a noogie and made away with the boots.

"What is it with this family and noogies?" Star smiled.

March 4

Snow-tipped trees painted a view outside of her bedroom window as the power inside Star grew and her body deteriorated. The cold weather subsided, but the snowflakes still sprinkled from the sky. They fell sporadically from the clouded sky, falling one by one like they were in a dance. Star hardly ever had to deal with the cold weather in the places she'd lived in. The way the snowflakes fell reminded her of the last Christmas she had spent with her father. She had wanted snow so badly on Christmas Day, but it never came. So after she had opened all of her gifts that were under the tree, he had her stand in the middle of the living room and close her eyes. When he prompted her to open them, little shimmering confetti fell from the sky. Her father stood over her and sprinkled them down from the staircase as she twirled in them. Oh, how she missed him.

She got up and went downstairs after she got dressed. Chenoa sat at the table eating breakfast with Jacy. "Good morning," she said, walking over to the fridge for some orange juice.

"I'm surprised you're up so early," Jacy laughed as he shoveled a spoonful of cereal into his mouth.

"Yeah, I'm kind of shocked myself."

"I want to go outside and play, Grandma," Chenoa called out to Ruth.

"Well, let me get you cleaned up, and maybe Jace will take you outside," she smiled and replied.

"I guess I can take you outside if Star will come with us."

Star finished her juice and placed the glass in the sink. "Oh, Jacy, why do that to her? I don't..."

"Come on, Star, look at this face," he said, holding Chenoa's chubby cheeks between his two fingers, mushing them. "You can't deny a face like this." He smiled.

"Okay," Star replied. "Let me put some real clothes on."

She went upstairs and threw on a sweat suit and her sneakers. She went back downstairs and headed outside with Jace and Chenoa, who had already started playing. Star opened the door and felt a little dizzy. She held on to the door panel to catch her balance. The dizzy spell only lasted for a moment, and then it went away. She closed the door behind her and joined in the fun.

They played in the snow that still lay on the ground until Chenoa wanted to play hide-and-go-seek with Star. She said that it was no fun with Jacy because he always found her.

"Okay, Chenoa, go and hide." Chenoa ran out into the woods while Star pretended to count. "She's so cute. I've always wanted a little sister. I guess she's the closest thing I'll ever come to having one," she said to Jacy. "I guess I better go and find her."

Star walked out into the forest and said, "I wonder where little Chenoa could be?" She walked past the brush and around trees, but couldn't find her. She began to grow tired, no, weak. She held on to a tree to catch her breath, but breathing wasn't the problem. She walked back toward the house, looking into the sun. Its light beamed through the trees. The sunlight didn't have the same effect on her anymore. She was able to stare into its light without it blinding her, only at that moment, its brilliant flare streaked across the sky, and everything went black.

Jacy stood from his seat on the deck when Chenoa returned from the forest without Star. "Where's Star, Chenoa?" he yelled.

"I don't know. She's still out there looking for me. I finally won. She's really bad at this game, Uncle Jace."

"Go in the house with Grandma, okay?" He opened the door for her and ran to find Star. He followed her scent until he found her lying in the snow, covered in snowflakes. He ran over to her and tried to wake her. He called out her name and tapped her face. When her eyes started to flutter, he said, "Wake up, Princess. What happened to you?"

Star strained to focus on his face and his question. "I...I don't know," she replied.

"Maybe this was a bad idea. You need your rest. Come on, I'll get you to bed." He picked her up and took her back to the house. The darkness took over Star before the door closed behind him.

✵ ✵ ✵

When Star awoke, she thought that she was still dreaming. The night sky shocked her. Had she really been sleeping all day? She rolled away from the window in disbelief and placed her hands under her face. A point in her bracelet grazed her cheek. She pulled her hand out and began to play with it between her fingers. It meant so much to her now. In a sense, it was as if she had gotten it from her father. She wondered what Jaelyn was actually like and if she was anything like her. She did love to dance, and according to Lucero, she had her eyes. She wondered what it would be like living in another world. To have the freedom to jump from the Earth and return to the sky. She heard a knock at the door and turned, untangling her covers, and sat up as the light flickered on. Kaya walked in with a tray of food.

"Hey sleepyhead, we thought you might be hungry."

Star cleared her throat. "How did you know I was awake?"

"Jace noticed that your breathing had changed. Nice having wolves around, huh?" Kaya laughed. "You gave him quite a scare earlier. Chenoa, on the other hand is still happy that she won." Kaya placed the tray over Star's lap saying, "Eat up. I'll come and get your dishes when you're done."

Star ate as much of the steak, potatoes, and peas that she could and placed the food aside. She hadn't realized that, when Kaya came in, all she wore was a cami and her underpants. Someone must have taken off everything that wasn't wet. She grabbed her housecoat and headed for the shower. When she came back to the room, the plate was gone. She walked over to the closet and pulled out a pair of flannel pj bottoms and a T-shirt Ruth had gotten for her. Ruth felt that one pair wasn't enough. They were black with rainbow-colored stars and white shooting stars all over them. The T-shirt had a single shooting star on the front. She had let Chenoa pick them out. Star was finally getting over the mere mention of shooting stars. Chenoa, even if she didn't know it, really made being there easier. She threw on a sweater and went downstairs. The night was still young, and she didn't want to go back to bed.

Everyone sat in the cozy living room watching a movie. There was no use for a fireplace, but Jacy always sat next to it reading a book or watching the TV. Star thought that it may be because he got tired of sleeping on the couch or because he didn't want to make Kaya and Chenoa too hot. Jessie and Ruth always got the two recliners that sat along the wall across from Jacy.

"Did you get enough rest?" Jessie inquired.

"Yes, I'm sorry about earlier," Star said as she twisted her ponytail in her hands.

"Oh, there's nothing to apologize for. We don't know how this thing is going to work, but we did know that there were going to be side effects. The good thing is that you're okay." He smiled.

Star curled up in the seat next to Jacy and whispered, "I'm really sorry. Kaya told me that I…"

"You heard the big guy. There's nothing to apologize for. Now watch the movie."

Star smiled. "So what are we watching anyway?"

"I don't know, some chick flick Kaya picked out about some guy falling for a girl that's already taken."

Star sat back and watched the movie as the night proceeded.

March 14

The snow began to melt away and the greenery in the forest began to poke its head through. The months that had gone by melted away as the pack waited to pounce on their unwanted guest. Star also awaited his arrival. She didn't know if she would cower away and ask that he be spared or be able to look him in the face as his life was taken away from him.

Her feelings ate at her, gnawing away at her thinning neck. She didn't understand why he had stayed away so long. Did she dream about what the pack had in store for him so he stayed away? Did she dream about being with the pack and that's what scared him away? Did she dream about Jacy?

While he stayed away, they continued to grow closer. Star would draw photos of Jacy and Chenoa playing while she sat on the deck. Kaya helped her with her hair and wardrobe, as she said the five dresses, dated tees, and her return to ponytails weren't working for a princess.

Her feelings weren't the only things that ate away at Star. As promised, the power ate away at her as well. She slept even more and didn't play with Chenoa as much as she used to. She was almost thankful for the snow melting away because it hurt her not to play in the snow with Chenoa. She didn't understand why Star was unable to join her, but Jacy made sure she had someone to play with. Star would join them from time to time, but usually found herself in bed for the rest of the day.

She didn't want anyone to see how it was affecting her, but it was becoming too hard to hide it. She blamed being weak on a loss of appetite. Though she didn't really crave food, it was the power that ate away her strength. Her power had grown, and though she enjoyed using it, she could tell that her excessive use only slowed her human body down. The power was too much for her to continue using, but when she saw Chenoa's smile, it was all worth it. She loved the stars, just like Starfire had as a child. Her deterioration didn't matter if for one more day she could see her smile, but there was one smile she had begun to miss.

March 16

Star awoke to find Jacy sitting on the bed beside her. His face hung in a sad smile as her eyes still focused to the lights. She sat up slowly and asked, "What's wrong?"

He drew in a deep breath and replied, "You've been out for two days."

"You're not serious, right?"

He leaned over and said, "I think that it's time for you to know."

"To know what?"

"Where you are."

Star's eyes widened in anticipation.

"You're in New York, just along the border of Erie County."

"I'm in New York? What made you tell me?"

"I'm telling you because I need you to dream, to dream about him. You're running out of time, and I don't know how much longer you have," Jacy said, touching her face. "You must still keep this information from your mother, and we still need for you to stay close to the house, as we'll probably only have one chance to catch him off guard."

Star nodded, and he handed her the phone. "You're mother has been calling. My dad says that you shouldn't worry her, so just tell her that you forgot to charge your phone. I'm going to give you a moment alone. Do you want Kaya to come and help you in the shower?"

Star shook her head no. Jacy stood up and sluggishly left the room. She pressed "1" on the phone and called her mother.

She answered on the second ring, "Star, honey, what happened to you? I've been calling and calling."

"Mom, I'm sorry. I...I forgot to charge my phone. I'm so sorry."

She spoke with her mother for half an hour, until her phone was really about to die. She placed it on the nightstand and slowly stepped out of bed. It took her a minute to steady herself, but she made her way to the bathroom to take her shower.

✧ ✧ ✧

Star headed downstairs in her sweatpants and T-shirt as the rumbling voices began to dissipate. She just wanted to turn around and go back to her room, but she couldn't. Though she knew they were concerned she didn't want them to fuss over her. The look on Jacy's face said enough.

"Good afternoon Star," Ruth greeted her at the end of the stairwell with a hug. She had never hugged her before. As Ruth pulled away, Star saw the whole family sitting at the kitchen table around one empty seat with a plate of food piled on it. Ruth pulled her over to the seat and pulled it out for her. "Look, I made your favorite, pancakes, and I added fruit with it as well. I know you're not going to eat it all, but just try." She walked around the table as Jessie stood up for her to sit down.

Star stared at the plate sitting in front of her and then looked up at the four onlookers. Her stomach didn't call out to her, but she knew that it needed to be fed. She picked up the fork and plunged it into the mound. She lifted a piece of the brown fluff and placed it in her mouth.

She couldn't take the quiet audience gawking at her, so she put her fork down and said, "So, how was everyone's morning?" She smiled. They all remained silent. "Seriously, you guys, I'm fine."

They all looked at her, not wanting to say what was on their mind. Jacy looked at her with his dark eyes crying out to her. No longer did she fear them. They had become warm and compassionate. They were the eyes she had started to dream of. But looking at them now, all she saw was torment and sorrow.

"It's our job to make sure you're okay, Star. It's what we were made for. I know that Jacy told you where we are and that you still need to stay close, but we're really going to need your help. Only you can lead him here. Only you can save your life now." Jessie looked down at Jacy and said, "We waited too long to tell you, but we see now the toll it's taken on you."

Star brushed her hair from her face. "I'm fine. Really, I am. I just needed to rest, that's all. I felt how much Jerick wanted to be with me and saw what he and his father had in store for us. There's no way he won't come looking for me."

Jacy got up from the table. He just couldn't take it anymore and went out the back door. Star jumped from her chair and ran to the door, but he was already gone, and his T-shirt and shorts lay in tattered pieces across the lawn. Star turned and slouched against the door as tears began to puddle in her eyes.

Kaya came over to her and hugged her arms around her. She wiped away her tears and pulled Star's face to hers and smiled. "Let's get some food in you."

Star only ate about a third of the plate while Kaya sat with her to keep her company. "What did I say, Kaya?"

"He's a boy, Star, a boy who's half wolf, who knows what sets them off."

"I can't eat anymore. Can I just save it for later?"

"Sure," Kaya responded. She took the barely eaten plate of food and wrapped it up for her.

Star's meals usually ended up the same way, wrapped up in the fridge, and then Ruth would throw them away by the following morning.

"Chenoa will be asleep for another hour or so. How about we get you outside for some fresh air?"

Star went upstairs to grab her jacket and then went outside to join Kaya on the deck. She sat down next to her and hugged her legs to her chest. "What happened, Kaya? Why did he run off? I know that you know more than you're letting on."

Kaya looked out into the wooded area and said, "I promised I wouldn't say anything, Star. But you have to know that you mean so much to him, and for some reason he feels responsible for what's happening to you."

"How could he feel responsible? This isn't his fault," Star said, lifting from her seat and holding stars in both hands. "We were both cursed with someone else's burden. It's no more his fault than anyone else around here." Tears fell from her crystal eyes as she turned to Kaya. "Where would he have gone?"

"I don't know, and besides, he's probably miles away from here."

"He couldn't have gone that far. Your father told everyone to stay close, remember?"

Kaya looked down because she knew that she was caught in her lie and tried to hide the fact that Jacy lingered just past the brush. "Give me a second, okay?"

Star nodded, and the burst of light evaporated from her hands.

Kaya returned with a pair of shorts and walked out into the woods. She returned and said, "Give him a moment, and then you can go. I'll be inside if you need me." Kaya then went back inside.

Star headed out to the woods, stuffing her hands in her pockets. The sun on her face felt good. She still couldn't believe how long she had slept. Sure, she felt a little tired, but that was normal for someone who hadn't moved around in two days, right?

Jacy stood staring up at the sky. Star walked up behind him slowly, but he didn't turn, so Star slid her hand in his and leaned against his arm. "Are you okay?" she asked, looking up at him as his eyes met hers.

"I'm okay. I just needed a moment to myself."

"Do you want me to leave?"

"No," Jacy replied, gaining a tighter grasp on her hand and turning to her. "I'm sorry."

"Ditto."

"What are you sorry for?"

"For making you worry about me." Star reached up to touch the side of his face. "I mean, we knew that there was going to be side effects. They can't all be good, right?"

Jacy stood still, holding her hand, not letting his eyes waver.

"You have to promise me that you won't blame yourself for whatever happens to me. I know that you consider me your responsibility, but it's like my mother told me before I left. Each of us has our own story to write, but only we're able to write it."

Jacy looked at her as a gust of spring air whisked hair across her face. He lifted his hands and wiped the hair away from her face. His rough hands still brought comfort to Star. Even though they no longer burned her, she still felt warm at his touch. *Is it his hands or the way they make me feel?* Star thought to herself.

Jacy replied, "If you promise me that after this is over..." Jacy paused and swallowed, unable to let what he wanted to say release from his lips. "After this is over, you have to promise me that we'll still be friends."

Star looked at him, uncertain as to why he would even need for her to make that promise. "You, the pack, and Kaya are technically the only friends I have. Of course we will." She smiled. Jacy opened his arms, and she jumped up into them.

March 17

Star stayed up late with Jacy and the pack, but still headed up to bed before they left. She knew that they were holding back that night, and she was thankful. She didn't know how Jacy was able to handle all of those people in his head when she had a hard enough time fighting with herself and the new power that was growing inside her. She felt it like the cold air that brushed her face during the winter or the warm air that blew from Jacy's mouth when he would talk to her. Deep down she was afraid of when it would completely take over. Would that be the day that she died? Would it be tomorrow or just wait until the day before her birthday? Jerick had to come before then. He had to.

Jacy heard as Star rustled in her sheets, so he left the pack to lock up and go to their posts. Cody and Poe took the night shift out in the woods, and Stephen hung around the woods during daylight, covering the whole area until they woke up to continue the next day.

"Are you awake, Princess?"

Star turned over and replied, "I can't sleep."

"Good," Jacy laughed and walked over. "I need to ask you something."

Star had brought forth a cascade of hanging stars behind her. They had grown accustomed to staying up to talk underneath the stars until she fell asleep.

"I need to ask you about something you wrote in your book," Jacy said as he sat at the end of her bed.

Star sat up and replied, "What is it?"

"What does Jerick have planned?"

"I don't understand. What are you talking about?"

"I mean, what does he have planned for you and him?"

Star crawled to the end of the bed and replied, "Jacy, I don't think..."

"Please, I want to know."

She took in a deep breath and looked out the window. "He showed me once a little while after I came here." She looked at Jacy and then back out the window. "A land that was empty as far as the eye can see. There was nothing but land. No buildings, no cars, no people, just he and I standing there. I looked up and saw the sun and the moon coexisting by one another in the sky. I couldn't tell the time of day. I looked down into Jerick's eyes that held nothing but sheer happiness. He said to me that this was our home now. All of it belonged to him and I. That it was our birthright. When I asked him what had happened to everyone, he told me that his mother had a way to make the Earth swallow all of its contents and rejuvenate itself. To cleanse itself from all that didn't belong. I screamed at him, wondering why, how he could do such a thing to them, to me. He told me that he hated humans. They destroyed his home and took me away from him time after time. I...I told him that I didn't belong to him and that the others chose their own lives to live. I told him that I hated him and never wanted to see him again."

Jacy sat there quietly, not knowing what to say. Star turned to look at Jacy and said, "He hasn't returned because of me. I pushed him away then, and I didn't try to help him when he said he was hurt."

Jacy wasn't sure if she was upset that he hadn't returned for her or because she may have lost her chance to survive. Either way, he couldn't just sit there and not say anything.

"He probably hasn't returned because we tore him to pieces," Stephen joked while Cody and Poe laughed.

Jacy also felt that may have been the reason, but he couldn't tell her. He was still unsure if she was really ready to lose Jerick or if she would be upset at what they had done. He pulled her over to him and hugged her. "I know he'll be back soon."

Star looked up at him and replied, "How do you know?"

"I know because if I were him, I wouldn't stay away."

Surprises

March 20

Kaya came to Star's room with her finger to her mouth, motioning for Star to be quiet. In her other hand she carried her laptop.

"More shopping?" Star sat on the bed next to Kaya as she opened her laptop showing a light pink sleeveless dress with a flared skirt.

Do you like it? she typed on a blank screen.

Star nodded yes and mouthed, "Why?"

She began to type again: *It's for Jacy's birthday.*

"Jacy's," was all that Star got out as Kaya motioned for her to be quiet again.

Jacy heard her, so he came upstairs to see what she wanted. "Did you need something?" Jacy asked as he opened the door to see the two of them on the bed. Star stuck Kaya's laptop behind her, while Kaya brushed Star's hair to try and play off what they were doing.

"Oh, I'm sorry. I didn't mean to call you."

Jacy laughed and went back downstairs.

Kaya stopped brushing when Jacy closed the door and tousled Star's hair for blowing their cover. She typed on the page that her mom was throwing Jacy a party for his birthday and that she wanted Star to have something new to wear.

So why are we sneaking around? Star wrote.

Because of this. Kaya clicked on another page to show a used black Land Rover. She typed: *He's been saving for a truck for years, and Mom and Dad told him that they would help him buy it, but they never told him when he would get it.*

Star turned the computer to her and wrote: *How is it a secret if your dad knows?*

He doesn't know. He never knows. Mom gets all of their gifts, remember?

Well what am I going to get him?

That's up to you, but you need to figure it out soon. I can take you to the store. Kaya beamed as she typed.

If she would've asked a couple of months ago, Star would've jumped at the invite, but she really didn't feel like it. She decided that she wanted to stay and wait for Jerick's arrival so that the whole thing could be over with. Star typed on her keyboard to get him a gift card for gas or stuff for the truck, something they could use on their road trip. She went to the closet and pulled out two hundred dollars from her bag. She typed on the computer again. *Do you think this is enough?*

Kaya nodded and said, "There's one more thing."

She pulled up another web page that had a pair of pink heels sitting on the page. "Oh no!"

"Come on, they'll look perfect with it."

"Yeah, just as nice as my flip-flops."

"Too late," Kaya said. "I was just showing them to you. I already placed the order for them as well as the dress. I just wanted to make you feel like you had a part in it." Kaya laughed and switched the page back to type: *This is going to be the best birthday he's ever had!*

March 27

Kaya helped Star get into her new pink dress that just fit. "It's a good thing I ordered it a size smaller. We're going to throw you a party like this when you turn eighteen. By then, we can even invite your mom and I'm going to make you eat every bit on your plate even if I have to tie you down to do it," she laughed. "You'll be back to normal in no time."

Star smiled, but didn't comment. She hoped that would all come true, but she was growing unsure, as she still had not been visited by Jerick. She hadn't noticed his absence before. He only visited her dreams, waiting on the sidelines until her father died. How had this man who once comforted her become someone she wanted back in her life, only to take his?

"Hey, are you okay?"

"Yeah, I'm sorry. I was thinking about something," Star replied.

She looked at Star from head to toe and said, "How freaked is Jacy going to be when he sees you?"

Star smiled and walked over to the dresser to comb her hair and put on some lip gloss.

"Here, let me," Kaya said, pulling out makeup and proceeding to apply it to Star's face. "We can't have you walking around with dark circles." She put down her brush and crossed her arm over her waist. "What should we do about the hair?" Kaya said as she tapped a finger on her glossed lip. "I know. Do you have a ponytail holder?"

She pulled a ponytail from her kit and gave it to Kaya.

"This will look so cute on you," Kaya said as she whisked Star's hair into a tight ponytail and twirled the curls around. She grabbed one of Star's hands and said, "Hold this here." She ran to Chenoa's room and came back holding hairpins. Chenoa followed her into the room with Bear in her arm. She wore a lavender skirt and T-shirt with butterflies fluttering around the collar.

Kaya took Star's hand off her head and stuck in one of the pins while she held the others in between her lips. She put in the rest of the pins and rubbed her fingers. "I guess I should've waited to put on my lip gloss." She smiled. "There. Do you like it?"

Star looked into the mirror, eyeing Kaya's work. "I like it!"

"I like it too, Mommy." Chenoa laughed as she stumbled over to them wearing Star's new shoes.

"Take those off, Chen. If you scuff her new shoes, I'm going to get you."

It was always funny to see Kaya discipline her because she did it with a smile on her face. Star laughed, "How is she ever going to take her seriously when you laugh?" She walked over and picked up the little girl from her shoes. "If I have to compete with the two of you for my shoes, I'm going to have to get Jacy on the both of you," she muttered, tickling Chenoa.

She slipped on her shoes and walked around to make sure she was comfortable with wearing them. "Do you think they're a little much? Maybe I should put my flats on."

"If you do, I will kill you, and Jacy would kill me. You don't want Chen to grow up without a mother, would you?" Kaya pouted and bent down, squeezing her face to Chenoa's.

"Okay, I won't change them, but we better get downstairs. It sounds like people are showing up."

"Wait, I think you need one more touch." Kaya reached down and took one of the butterflies Chenoa had cascading in her hair and placed it on the side of Star's curly bun. "Now you're ready. I have to redo my makeup. I want to look great for the pictures," she replied as she ran to her room.

Star walked over to the bed and grabbed the white shrug that she had borrowed from Kaya, bent down to Chenoa. "I guess we should head on down then. Shall we?" Star said as she reached out her hand. Chenoa placed her hand in Star's, and they went. She still felt a little insecure, but everyone else was probably going to be dressed up as well. Chenoa jumped down the final step, causing Star to lose her footing. She felt an arm reach around her from the back and catch her before she fell.

Jacy looked down at her, smiling. "Gotcha," he said in his deep voice. "I'm guessing Kaya picked out the shoes?"

Star smiled, and he placed her back on her feet. "Thanks," she replied, looking down at her clothes. "Actually, the whole ensemble was her idea."

"Wow, she can do something right!" He smiled as she blushed and pushed him away. Jacy gave way to her push.

"Happy birthday."

"Thank you. Do I get a birthday kiss?" he asked with a coy smile.

"Sure." Star shrugged and called out, "Chenoa, your uncle wants a birthday kiss!"

Chenoa happily obliged and ran over to her uncle, who lifted her in his arms for a kiss. "Happy birthday, Uncle Jace!" she said with her high-pitched voice.

"Thank you," he replied, putting her down and nudging Star. "No fair using the kid."

Star laughed, and she headed over to help Ruth finish. Jacy went into the living room with their houseguests.

☆ ☆ ☆

Everyone was there, and Jacy was the happiest he had been in months. Star was so happy to finally see a lasting smile on his face. He seemed to fake a lot of them lately. She also had a hard time creating a smile on her face after she realized that Kaya had tricked her into dressing up, because no one else had. But she hardly had any time to stress, because Chenoa kept her on her toes begging Star to show Myra her new star formations. Kaya and Cadee were able to pull her away now and again, but Chenoa always found her. She called Star her best friend. She didn't mind it since she didn't really have one of those anyway. Well, she could consider Jacy her best friend. He did know just about everything about her, and he was always there for her. She just wasn't sure if they would've been as close if they weren't forced to spend as much time with one another. She was almost happy that she had come there, aside from leaving her mother behind and the whole dying thing.

☆ ☆ ☆

"I still can't believe he hasn't contacted her yet," Cody said as he gulped down his fourth can of pop. "What is he waiting for?"

"I don't know," Jacy replied while he watched Star playing with Chenoa and Myra. "He only has two more months, but we have no idea how much more time she has."

"You haven't asked her about him lately. Maybe she's holding back on something," said Poe.

"She wouldn't do that," Jacy said, trying to hide how upset he was at his statement. "Besides, she wants to live just as much as I want her to, even if it's not for the same reasons. She wouldn't hold back something that could save her." His eyes never moved, and his voice stayed stern so that Poe and the rest of the pack wouldn't ask that question again.

✵ ✵ ✵

Jessie called out to everyone at the party that it was time to give Jacy his gift. They all gathered around the deck to see it, but his mom was nowhere to be found. Jessie looked at Kaya. "Where's your mother, Kay? She told me to gather everyone out back ten minutes ago."

Kaya shrugged her shoulders, when they heard a horn beeping in the driveway. One by one, they moved to the front of the house and saw the shiny black Land Rover sitting in the driveway with Ruth behind the wheel. Jacy rushed over, screaming in disbelief. She stepped out of the jeep, and Jacy wrapped his arms around her, lifting her off of her feet.

"This is awesome. Thank you! Thanks, Dad."

Jessie smiled, knowing that he had had no idea what the gift was going to be. Ruth walked over and hugged him around his waist.

"I thought you were going to wait until next year?"

"If I did, it wouldn't have been a surprise." She smiled, and Jessie leaned down to kiss her.

The pack had already found seats in the car for themselves, while Jacy marveled at the interior.

"We have to go somewhere, Jacy!" Cody spastically yelled out.

"Where?" Jacy asked. "It's getting late. Just about everything is closing."

Stephen turned to him with his eyes open wide. "Niagara Falls. We can drive up to the American side."

"But we can't just leave the party."

"Yes, we can. Everyone will be leaving soon anyway," Poe said, checking out the amenities in the back.

"Okay, on one condition."

"We know. I'll go and get her," Cody said while he got out of the truck.

"Aw, man, back there with them?" Stephen replied. Before Jacy could get the words out, he heard Jacy telling him to get in the backseat with the other guys.

"Yeah, I'll make it up to you," Jacy replied.

Star walked over to the truck with Cody and was greeted by Stephen, who held the door open for her to get in on the passenger side. "My lady," he said, bowing to her.

Star smiled and curtsied. "Why thank you, sir."

Cody helped her inside and hopped in next to Stephen.

"So do you like it?" she asked Jacy.

"I love it! So how long did you know about it?"

"About a week." She smiled.

"So are you ready for our first road trip?"

"Really? Now? But the party."

"It's okay," Cody replied. "Jessie said it was okay."

Star looked out the window and saw Jessie and Ruth still holding on to one another, waving good-bye.

"To the falls we go!" Jacy revved up the engine and drove off.

✫ ✫ ✫

It was funny watching three guys who looked too big for a recliner sitting in the back of a vehicle. Star asked Jacy to pull over so that one of them could sit in her seat, but they said that they were fine. Stephen was satisfied just to be able to play with the radio. His long arm would reach forward, changing the radio every five or ten minutes.

She was happy to be able to leave the house. Jacy said that she looked like a dog hanging out the window. She couldn't help but to look up at the night sky woven with stars that blanketed them by the time they reached the falls. The pack exited the truck, stretching their long limbs. Stephen walked over and opened the door for Star. The sound of the rushing falls welcomed her to their view. She couldn't believe how beautiful it was. She walked over to Jacy, who was waiting for her on the other side of the truck.

"This is amazing!" Jacy took her hand and walked her over to the rail. "Thanks for bringing me with you guys."

"I wouldn't have had it any other way."

"I told you this was a good idea, Jace! I can't believe you've never seen them before, cuz. Stick with us, and we can bring you here quicker than the Land Rover." He laughed and nudged Star.

She laughed. "It is truly amazing."

"One day we'll take you down underneath the falls," said Jacy.

"You can do that?"

"Oh yeah, they have a whole tunnel and everything. It's really cool," Cody replied.

Cody walked away to join Stephen and Poe, who had walked to another viewing point.

"So did you have a nice birthday?"

"It's the best one I ever had!" Jacy replied while he looked out into the mist from the falls.

"Looks like I'm rubbing off on you."

"What?" Jacy replied, regaining his attention.

"You're lost in your thoughts. What were you thinking about?"

"Oh, ah, nothing," Jacy said as he released his hand from hers and wrapped them around the railing.

"Are you okay?"

"I'm fine. I just have a lot on my mind."

"Well, I'm here. You always ask me to open up to you? Why don't you open up to me?"

"It's not something I can talk about."

"What do you mean? Does it have to do with Jerick?"

"What would make you think that? Do you miss him?" Jacy turned and almost yelled the question, startling other sightseers.

"Jacy, I didn't say that. Why won't you tell me what's wrong?"

The pack could tell that Jacy had grown upset and could read what he was thinking. He didn't care about the mission anymore. He just wanted to be with her, and he wanted to tell her exactly how he felt. They were so close? What if he never got a chance to tell her how he felt. He could never forgive himself.

He placed his hand on her face. Star could see that he was about to kiss her. She leaned in closer and closed her eyes, but nothing happened.

Jacy saw the pack approaching, and he removed his hand from her face. "It's time for us to go," was all he said.

Star opened her eyes and saw the look in his eyes. She couldn't make out what was happening. His hand released the rail beside them, leaving behind his handprint carved in the iron. He reached over, grabbing her hand, and brought her to the truck. The pack filed into the SUV. Jacy put the keys in the ignition and drove off. Star couldn't even look at him. She was so embarrassed. She took off her shoes and curled her legs underneath her dress while she looked out the window. She tried to hide the pain from them, but the lump inside her throat yanked her tears out. They fell like the waterfalls that grew smaller and smaller as they drove away. The ride was only about a half an hour long, but Star couldn't stop the sleep that fell upon her.

When they got back to the house, Jessie had already told Ruth about the near mishap. Jacy carried Star into the house and took her upstairs. He came back down upset that he had almost lost control in a public place and almost kissed Star. He couldn't bear the look on his father's face, especially since he already knew what was coming.

Jessie sat at the table and looked up at Jacy. "I know that you already know what I have to say, but I'm going to say it anyway. You know what's at stake and that you can't lose your control. What were you thinking? Don't answer that. I know how you feel, but she only has about two months left. What if he never comes back and she, God forbid...? You will be heartbroken. Isn't it better that you don't fall for her and she doesn't fall for you?"

"You should know that I'm already there, Dad," Jacy replied as he sat down and placed his head in his hands.

"You have to stay focused. I can't stop love, but neither can you. She may still choose him. Have you ever thought about that? Just try to make her time here the best you possibly can and know that your heart isn't the only one in jeopardy."

✲ ✲ ✲

"Where is everyone?" Star walked around searching. She wore a tattered wedding gown adorned in lace and floral finishings. Her veil tangled in her hair when she began to run, but she couldn't find anyone. "Jacy," she called out. "Where are you?" She stopped as loneliness crept into her mind. She hated being alone.

Then, from behind, she heard a faint voice calling her name. "Jacy, is that you?" she cried out, but no one came, so she ran toward the voice. Her feet scraped against the uncut grass that brushed at her ankles. She ran and ran, but she still could not find the source of the voice. "What's going on?" Star screamed out as desperation took over her. She fell in the grass filled with oxalises and wept.

She didn't know how much time had passed. The color in the sky had not changed from its light blue and lavender haze. The warm breeze that nestled her hadn't changed either, and still Star was alone. She sat up with her knees to her chest and buried her face in her arms.

I must be dead. This must be my own hell. I don't ever remember reading about personal afterlife quadrants where you experience all of your worst fears. Star looked toward the heavens for some type of answer, for something that made sense. When she looked up to the sun and the moon, they hung amongst the stars that lay dormant in the sky like they had lost their reason for existing. Star suddenly realized where she was. The earth was no longer dark and unwelcoming, but it was still...

"Home," a voice from the distance called out.

Star stood up and turned around, but no one was there. When she turned back, she saw Jerick.

"No, this isn't my home."

"Yes, it is," Jerick replied and wiped away her tears. "My parents came through for us, Star. It's all ours."

Star shrugged away, shaking her head.

"Now don't be upset. I had to make you miss me. That's why I stayed away. You've missed me, haven't you?"

Star walked away and began to run, but Jerick was faster. He grabbed her from behind and brought her down to the ground, causing her veil to come unpinned and fly away.

"Please don't fight me on this, Star. Don't you understand that all of these years of hurt and longing for you to be by my side was for this moment? Eternity was promised to me, and I can't imagine it without you."

Tears began to stream down Star's face. Jerick gazed into her eyes and leaned down to kiss her. His mouth encircled hers, forcing her mouth open with his tongue. His hands released from her wrist, traced down her neck, and moved down her chest. Star began to lose herself in him. His body pressed into hers while his hand reached down her thigh.

"Let me in, Princess," Jerick whispered in her ear.

His hand began to move up her thigh. His touch was so soft. It was like silk brushing against her skin. Star had never felt that way before. Jerick slowly pulled down the straps of her gown, when something in Star snapped. Her mind circled in fury when she realized it wasn't the taste of him that she longed for. It was Jacy's hands, his mouth, his touch that she wanted. She pushed him away and said, "No."

Jerick looked into her glistening eyes, confused at her reaction. His blue eyes still pierced Star's stomach like a sharp knife, grinding away at her flesh. "It's our destiny, Starfire. We were meant to be together. Don't you understand that?" He sat up and ran his hand through his dark hair to hide his tears from her.

Star sat silently at his reaction. She stood up, afraid to say anything.

Jerick turned to her and wiped the black liquid from his eyes. "It's him, isn't it? *Isn't it?*" he screamed. Star was too shaken to answer. "Well, we won't have to worry about your dark guardian much longer."

Star suddenly realized that she was only sleeping and that he was talking about Jacy. *How did he know?* she asked herself. "Jerick, please, I..."

"Enough. I have put up with the Night Howlers for far too long."

"Jerick," Star called out. "Please don't hurt them. They told me where I am. You can find me now. I'm..."

"I'm well aware of your location. I figured out the vicinity you were in and have already tried to come to you." He thought of his last attempt, where they tore him apart, causing him to stay away thus far. "I grow tired of their games and intrigues."

"Well, please tell me what to do? I'll do anything you want. Just please don't hurt them."

Jerick walked over and placed his hands on her cheeks. He looked into her eyes and said, "What I want is for you to be with me, but to spare his life, I need you to come to me. I promise I will not hurt him."

"I will come to you. Just let me know where you are," Star grabbed his hands and begged. He stood silent.

"You would allow everyone on Earth to perish just so that this...this Jacy can survive." He pulled his hands away. More black liquid streamed down his face. "The Night Howlers and every one of the soulless beings traipsing across our home will be destroyed!"

✲ ✲ ✲

"Star, snap out of it," Jacy screamed, trying to shake her awake. Sparks began to shoot from her hands, bursting against the walls. He took her face in his hands and said, "You have to hear me. This is Jacy. Please, please, wake up."

Jessie raced upstairs with the fire extinguisher to put out the fire on the walls and pulled the window open. A burst of air blew through the room, floating the foam around like snowflakes.

Jacy still sat holding Star's face in his hands. "Please wake up," he said with tears pooling in his eyes.

Star could hear him calling her, pulling her from Jerick's view. His eyes focused on her with anger. Jerick uttered two words before she lost his sight. She couldn't hear him, but she read his lips: "You're mine."

"No!" Star screamed as her eyes popped open. Her crystal eyes shed shimmering tears down her cheeks and onto Jacy's hands. It took her a moment to focus, but when she was able to see, Jacy was still there. Tears had begun to stream down his face at the sight of her consciousness. She wrapped her arms around him as her body shook and fell limp around his shoulders. She couldn't stop crying.

"He's coming!" she screamed, holding on to Jacy with all of her strength. She breathed in deeply, repeating the words over and over again.

Jacy stroked her hair to try to calm her down. "It's okay," he said.

His mother walked into the room just as the light flakes from the extinguisher fell to the ground.

Ruth came to comfort her, but Jessie pulled her back to make sure the swarm of shooting stars was over. "He's got it under control, honey. Can you go and get her some water?"

Ruth nodded while she inspected the damage to the room, then headed downstairs.

Jacy waited until her breathing calmed down and pulled Star from around his neck. He laid her limp body back down on the bed and brushed the fallen hair away from her face. "Now tell me what happened."

Star placed her hands over her face and began to cry. "Please don't ask me to."

Jessie walked over and placed his hands over hers to pull them down. "We need to know," he said with his deep voice.

She looked up at him and said, "He told me that he was coming for me and that everyone was... everyone wa..." She couldn't get the rest out.

Her hands flew back to her face as she rolled over into her pillow. Jacy rubbed her back. He could feel the bones protruding from beneath her skin.

"I'll be downstairs," Jessie said and left the disheveled room.

"It's okay, Princess. You don't have to worry. If he comes anywhere near you, we'll kill him first. Did you tell him about the dagger?"

"No," Star mumbled into the pillow.

"See? We're fine." He pulled at her shoulder and brushed her hair away.

Ruth came in with a glass of water. "You're probably really thirsty. Here you go. I'll go and start dinner."

Star drank some of the water, but her hands were too weak to hold the glass, so Jacy helped her until she was done. He placed the glass on the nightstand. "Here, you should lie back down," he said as he lowered her back down on the bed.

She started to calm down. Her body melted against him, and she was finally able to comprehend what Ruth had said. "I must have been really tired to have slept until dinnertime."

Jacy looked away and then back into her eyes that still held a puddle of tears. They reminded him of a full moon hanging over a lake at midnight. He sighed and said, "It's been longer than that, Princess. It's April first."

April 6

The destruction in Jacy's room left dark smudges and holes all over the walls. Star promised to help him paint it whenever this was over. She felt so embarrassed at what she had done that she spent most of her time sulking in her room. She also used that as an excuse to stay away from Jacy. She couldn't believe that she thought he was trying to kiss her. He seemed like he wanted it just as much as she did. She sat on the bed, drawing them at the falls, remembering the way the water flowed down and pummeled everything that lay beneath. It was so powerful and beautiful. How could something so beautiful be so deadly? She looked down at her notebook and saw that she had drawn Jerick's eyes over the picture of her and Jacy. She threw the book down and put her head on her fist.

Jacy ran up to the room and knocked on the door. "Are you okay?"

"Oh yeah, I'm fine," Star replied and straightened up on the bed.

He walked into the room and said, "You know, it's nice out. Why don't you go and get some fresh air?"

"I don't want to," she replied and got up to pick up her book off of the floor. She placed it in the closet and went to sit on the bed, but when she turned around, Jacy was standing with her flip-flops in his hands.

"I don't want to make you come out with me, but you are looking really pale these days. I think some sun will help you feel better, maybe have a little fun, you know, live a little."

"I feel fine, maybe twenty pounds lighter, but fine." She smiled, looking down at her frail arms and concave stomach.

"Don't make me carry you."

"Okay, okay, give me my shoes."

Jacy handed them over, and they headed outside. Star had to admit, the sun did feel good on her skin. She hadn't been outside since Jacy's party, and she had been missing the smell of the woods as the spring air flowed in.

"See, I told you, you needed some fresh air."

"Oh, whatever."

They walked in the woods for a little while until they stopped so that Star could rest.

"Do you want me to carry you back?"

"No, I just need a minute." She sat down on the grass and then decided to just lie down.

"You know, when you came, I didn't picture you as a wildlife type of person," Jacy said, lying down next to her.

"Well what kind of girl did you think I was going to be, some stuck-up snob?"

Jacy laughed and said, "Yeah, you got it right on the nose." He rolled over on his side and propped his head up with his hand. "Can I ask you something?"

Star turned to her side and propped herself up. "Anything."

"Why is it that this whole time you've only allowed me to call you Princess?"

Star paused and lay back down. "I guess I never noticed."

"You're lying to me."

"No, I'm not," she replied as she rolled over on her stomach and propped herself up on both arms, glaring over at Jacy.

"Yes, you are," he responded and leaped away so quickly that Star hardly saw him leave. She jumped up and circled around, trying to see where he went. There was no trace of him. The grass hadn't even crushed beneath his feet. Suddenly her shadow became eclipsed by a figure standing behind her. She turned around and saw Jacy, in wolf form, standing on his hind legs, looking down at her.

"What was that?" she asked the big wolf, folding her arms. He stepped back, bending down, and placed his humanlike paw out for her to climb on. She cocked her head to the side, smiled, and climbed on, leaving her flip-flops abandoned on the forest floor.

✭ ✭ ✭

At dinner Ruth watched Star push her food from side to side on her plate. Whenever she saw her looking, she would take a bite just to satisfy her.

Kaya had kept her occupied with talking about work so that she didn't have to think about how much she didn't understand guys, until she said, "So what did you guys do today? Mom told me you finally left the house."

"Yeah, I had to threaten her, but I was finally able to get her out." Jacy laughed at his achievement.

"So what did you do?" Kaya asked Star.

"We just walked around, and I went for a ride. I mean I rode on Jacy. I mean he gave me a ride in the woods. Okay, I don't know how to say it, but you get the picture."

"I think that's the reddest I've ever seen your face Star," Jessie said, causing a thunder of laughter throughout the room.

✲ ✲ ✲

Star gave up her kitchen duties since she had grown so weak. She was too afraid that she might drop something. She joined the family on the couch while Jacy cleaned the kitchen. Stephen stopped by to hang out with him and lent a hand.

"I would've thought that he would've shown himself by now. What is he waiting for?" Stephen questioned his fellow pack member as he swept, using his inside voice.

"I don't know, but she doesn't have much longer. This thing inside her is slowly eating her away," replied Jacy.

"Tell me about it. I think Chenoa is darker and weighs more than she does." Stephen laughed, but realized that Jacy found no humor in his comment. "I'm sorry. I shouldn't have been so insensitive."

"It's okay. It's true. It explains why she's always tired and hardly ever eats, but I don't think that's why she's been so distant."

"You know just as well as I do why she's so distant. She's hurt. Sleeping for almost four days is not going to make a girl forget when she's been turned down," Cody responded, roaming around outside.

"Do you really think that's it?"

"Man, you really need to get out more," Poe replied.

"Hey, we weren't talking to either of you," scolded Jacy.

"Maybe not, but I do know Cadee. If she's anything like the rest of the girls in our family, she hasn't forgotten."

"What's all this chitter-chatter about, girls?" Grandpa Joe asked.

"Oh, nothing, Grandpa, sorry to wake you."

A deep rumble of laughter rolled in Jessie's chest. All of the girls were left puzzled because there wasn't anything funny happening on TV. Jacy and Stephen burst out laughing as well and finished cleaning the kitchen.

✲ ✲ ✲

Nightfall seemed to come early that night. The sky turned gray and faded to black as rain gushed from the sky. The pitter-patter of raindrops on the window always helped Star sleep, but she just could not go to sleep. She lay silent in bed, staring at the ceiling, wondering why Jerick hadn't come yet. Why would he have said what he said, only for him to wait even longer? She had begun to grow impatient. She missed her old life, with her mother dancing around the kitchen, making cookies, and seeing her smile when her mom used to watch movies that her mom didn't like but she watched them with her anyway. She wanted to tell her mom that she was okay, but her mom knew the truth now. When she hadn't woken up in two days, Jacy answered the phone and told her about the power she had obtained and how it took a lot out of her. Star could tell the torture she was experiencing by her voice when she was finally able to call her. The memory made a lump grow in Star's throat.

She put aside her thoughts and decided that she didn't want to think about things that made her sad, or Jerick, anymore. She just wanted to be free. She wanted to dance. Star slowly pulled back her covers and placed her bare feet down on the ground. She slowly slid off of the bed. She tiptoed over Jacy and to the door, but as she opened it, Jacy popped up and grabbed the door with his right hand and her hand with the left.

"Where are you going?"

Star turned and smiled. "I'm going to bathe in the moonlight!"

"What?"

"You can come with me if you want to," Star whispered and smiled.

Jacy let go of the door, and they tiptoed downstairs. He opened the door, and Star turned to give him one last invitation. "Someone once told me to live a little. You should take their advice."

She ran out into the rain and allowed the gifts from the sky to drench her. She threw out her arms and raised them to the sky as the rain matted her hair to her face and back. Her nightgown clung to her body like a wet suit. Luckily she wore her purple one, so it wasn't see-through, but it showed all of her curves, making Jacy blush as he watched her from the door. She was so happy. The smile on her face wrenched his stomach into a bunch of knots. He hadn't seen that smile since she saw the falls. The falls was all he could think about, and the one moment that she actually wanted to kiss him. She wanted him.

Star twirled and twirled until she made herself a little dizzy. Jacy raced over and grabbed her like he had when she was falling down the stairs, but this time he held on.

"Jacy," Star said, confused because her footing only faltered, but she wasn't falling. She placed her hand on his bare chest. "Your heart is beating so fast. I thought you guys didn't get tired?"

"That's not why it's beating so fast," Jacy replied with his deep voice that seemed to be shaking.

Jacy ran his hand along the side of her face and brought his lips down to hers. She held his arms and lost herself in them as his hands lost all sense of composure. They went down her back and grazed her breast when he reached again for her face. Star had never felt anything like it before. What she had felt when Jerick touched her didn't compare to what she was feeling now. It was pure, unbridled ecstasy. It conjured up the being inside of her as her arms wrapped around his neck. But just as the spark built up inside her, he pulled away.

"I'm sorry, Princess. I...I need to get you back to bed." His rain-drenched hair hung over his face, but his eyes looked away in the forest. He picked her up and took her inside. He left his shoes at the door and carried her upstairs. His heart still thumped uncontrollably. He turned on the light and dropped her off in the bathroom. While he still refused to look at her, he said with a trembling voice, "My mother will kill me if you catch a cold, so you better dry off and get under the covers." Just before he closed the door, he grabbed a towel and looked at her with those tortured eyes Star hated seeing on his face. "Goodnight Princess."

Star stood shocked, confused, and hurt beyond belief. She looked down at her dirty feet as water streamed from her nightgown, making lines in the mud. She climbed into the shower without even removing her gown, turned on the water, and sat in the corner crying.

Kaya walked into the bathroom and pulled back the curtain. "How long have you been in here?"

"I...I don't know," Star replied, looking at her wrinkled fingers.

"Come on out," Kaya replied and reached over to turn off the water. She grabbed a towel to dry her off. "I swear the two of you are going to be the death of me."

"Where is he?" asked Star.

She hesitated to answer, but she felt that there was no reason to lie. "He's outside. Cody came in to watch over you and heard you in here crying for some time, so he woke me up. What's going on?"

Star couldn't respond. She didn't know what to say. She didn't have anything else to say. Words couldn't form to describe what she was feeling.

Kaya realized that she wasn't going to get anything out of her tonight, so she helped her get on some new pajamas and left her to sleep.

April 7

Star's eyes felt like they were welded shut from all of their puffiness. She curled up under her covers and stared at the blotches that now painted the walls like polka dots. She still couldn't believe what had happened that night, but she really couldn't believe what had happened last night. The feeling inside her was stronger than she could've imagined. His touch was more than she could've imagined. *Why did he push me away?* she thought to herself, sobbing into her blankets. It was karma for hurting Jerick. She had seen it in a movie once. They said, *"You reap what you sow."* She tossed in her sheets, leaving behind patches of glittered tears, and fell back to sleep.

She felt a nudge on her shoulder and woke up.

"Do you plan on sleeping all day?" Kaya asked Star. "You look like you want to sleep forever. You look like death, Star. What happened?"

Star rolled over and covered her head with her blanket.

"Okay, you won't tell me, but you need to get up."

Star replied, "No, I don't want to."

"Oh, come on, Mom can make anything you want to eat. Even if all you want is a plate full of cookies, she'll do it."

Star didn't budge.

"Okay, I'm leaving, but you can't stay under those covers forever," said Kaya as she hung her head and left.

April 11

Star held her ground and didn't leave her room unless she had to go to the bathroom or needed to take a shower. Though she felt weak, hunger pains didn't come, and as long as they could still hear her moving around upstairs, they knew she was okay. Jessie had bolted the window again, so they didn't have any fear of her leaving out the window. Jacy had taken the night shift, so he hardly ever came home.

Star went to take shower for the morning, and when she got out, she heard Chenoa tell Kaya that the water had stopped. She got dressed and opened the door. Kaya was standing in front of her with her comb and brush.

"I'm not letting you out of here until I comb out your hair and you tell me why you're living like the living dead."

Kaya pushed her back into the bathroom and told Chenoa to go downstairs with Grandma while she and Star handled some business. She made Star sit on the toilet lid and combed out her hair.

"I'm so glad you washed your hair this morning. That saved me at least one step." She pulled the blow-dryer out of the cabinet, picked up the brush, and got down to work. About a half an hour later, Kaya put the dryer down and said, "Okay, you don't have the blow-dryer as an excuse anymore. I want to know what happened between you and Jace."

"Kaya, I really don't want to talk about that."

"Oh, come on, it might help."

Star hung her head and said, "We kissed."

"Are you serious? He finally did it."

"What do you mean, finally?"

"I guess I can say it now since the cat is out of the bag and Jace already broke the rules anyway."

"What? Why?

"First things first, Jace has wanted to be with you since the first day he saw you, but because of what happened with your great-grandmother, Dad thought it wasn't such a good idea. He didn't want the pack to make the same mistake by not protecting 'The Last Starfire,'" she said while using air quotes. "I guess, according to Dad, Jacy's feelings were

so strong for you that even Grandpa Joe got tired hearing about it."
She laughed. "The whole time he fought the urge to tell you, but he
wasn't sure if you felt the same way or if you were in love with Jerick.
I told him that he was crazy and that you were absolutely, positively
head-over-heels crazy about him but you just wouldn't admit it. I guess
something happened the night of his birthday, which I want to hear all
about, and that's when he knew that you felt the same way."

Star's eyes began to well with tears.

"Oh, don't cry. I didn't mean to upset you." She grabbed some
tissues and handed them to Star. "He'll come back. I know he will. He's
just really upset with himself for not waiting like Dad told him to. His
instructions were to protect you and to keep you happy. Dad felt—"

"I was happy."

"When? When you were lying in bed or wandering around your
room looking like the bride of Frankenstein?"

"Oh, shut up, Kaya. This is crazy. If I could just talk to him, I could
tell him that I am happy. That being together won't mess anything up."

"I don't think that's going to work. I've never seen him like this
before. It's worse than the first time you wouldn't wake up."

"Wait. Pump the brakes You've seen him."

"Oh yeah, I...ah..."

"Come on, Kay, tell me!"

"Well, he comes and checks in on you when you're sleeping, but
don't tell him I told you. I've told you too much already. Wait right
here, okay?" She left the bathroom, almost tripping over the cord to
the hair dryer, leaving Star shocked and upset.

It made Star remember one night where she gazed out the window,
trying to forget how upset she had been feeling. She thought that she
had seen smoke coming from the trees. It looked like the nose of one
of the wolves protruding from the branches, but her vision was blurred
by the tears in her eyes.

Kaya returned with lip gloss and a tiara. "I think that this will look
amazing on you. It's from my wedding, but I think it will bring you
more luck than it brought me." She placed the tiara on top of Star's
head and told her to pucker up. Kaya dabbed lip gloss on her lips and
said, "Now there's a princess."

Star got up and looked in the mirror. She had neglected to look in
the mirror for days because looking into her eyes made her situation
more apparent. The sparkle in her eye reminded her of when her life
had changed forever. Meeting Felix was just the beginning, because
after she met Lucero, there was no turning back. She slowly raised her

eyes and looked into the mirror. She couldn't believe what she saw. She had totally forgotten how upset she was at Kaya for not telling her about Jacy. She hadn't worn her hair straight in years. Kaya had done it so that it was straight, but curled on the ends. The tiara sat on top of her head in front of a little bump.

"Thank you, Kaya, I love it!" She turned around and wrapped her arms around Kaya's neck.

Kaya hugged her thin frame and sighed. "Come on, we have to get some food in you. I know you may not want to eat, but today I am not taking no for an answer."

Star helped Kaya clean up the bathroom as much as she could and headed to her room to get dressed. She put on the dress that her mother had gotten her for her birthday last year and tied a ribbon around her waist to help it fit. Before she could leave the room, Kaya was back.

"Felix is downstairs. He says that he's here to get you."

"But I don't understand. Aren't I the safest with you guys? I don't want to go."

"You have no choice. I have to help you pack your things. Listen to me," Kaya said as she grabbed Star's moist chin with her hand, "once this is over, you can come back, okay? Stop crying, and help me pack your things."

Star's strength was leaving her with every word that left Kaya's mouth. She didn't really help Kaya pack. She was too upset. Cody headed upstairs to see if she was ready so that he could bring down her bags. Kaya had to help Star down the stairs because her legs struggled to move beneath her. They protested against Felix, but Star's mouth could not. Felix was surprised to see her sunken state and rushed over to her.

"Are you okay, Princess? You look like you haven't eaten in days."

"I'm okay, but I don't want to leave."

"I'm sorry, but you have to. It's for the best. You should say your good-byes."

Star trembled as she walked over and hugged Ruth. Kaya stayed close to steady her. Her body had become so thin that Ruth was afraid to hug her because she thought that she would hurt her. She could not lift Chenoa, so she bent down to her and kissed her on her forehead.

"I don't want you to go, Star," she said as she wiped away a tear.

"Don't cry." Star wiped away her tears.

"You are," the smart little girl replied as everyone started to laugh.

Star wiped away her own tears and said, "This is only good-bye for now. I'll see you again soon. I promise." She hugged Chenoa and relied on Kaya to help her stand up.

She looked at Jessie and slowly walked over as she built up the courage to ask, "Is there any way?"

Jessie already knew what, rather whom, she was referring to. "He knows and is on his way."

Felix grabbed her hand. "It's time to go." He brought her outside and headed toward the car.

"But I can't leave without saying good-bye," Star pleaded as she tried to drag her feet.

"I don't quite understand the urgency, Felix," said Jessie.

"He's near," Felix replied.

"We haven't sensed him, but if he is, you can stay and fight. We have the dagger now. This will put an end to her suffering."

"Really? Where is it?"

Jacy came out of the house with Stephen and Poe, holding the dagger wrapped in the cloth. "I have it right here." He walked to Felix and handed it to him as he looked at Star.

Star released Felix's hand and turned to face Jacy. "Why did you leave?"

"It doesn't matter right now, Princess. Only your safety does."

"That's right. Now let's go."

Star stood in front of Jacy, staring at him. She turned around to Felix and said, "I'm not leaving without him."

"Star," Jacy almost whispered.

"What's going on here?" Felix asked, waving his hand.

"I don't want to leave without him," she turned and said sternly as her legs wobbled beneath her.

Jacy looked down at her, and in a split second she saw Felix plunge the dagger into Jacy's heart. Jacy fell down to the ground. A wall of fire burst in between them and everyone else, almost burning Cody where he stood. Star fell to the ground with him and curled over to see the blood ooze from the gaping wound in his chest. She tried to cover his wound and felt his heart stop beating. Tears streamed down her face as she bent over, whispering something in his ear. Everything went dark, and she slumped down beside him.

Felix still held the dagger in his hand as the wall of fire held the Night Howlers at bay. They had transformed into their wolf beings, but could not get past the blazing wall. He could hear their angry growls between the flickers of the flame. He pulled Star away from Jacy, lifted her frail, blood-soaked body into the car, and drove away.

The wall slowly dissipated into the wind as the pack transformed back to their human selves, not caring about their nudity, and ran to their fallen brother. Jessie stormed over and stood above his son. He knelt down beside him and wiped blood and the tears Star had left behind off of his face while Ruth sat crumpled on the ground, crying with Kaya. Chenoa was sobbing in Grandpa Joe's arms. He had raced over after the rest of the pack arrived, and now wished he had waited, because he may have been able to stop Felix before he drove away with Star.

"My son!" Jessie cried out as he picked up his limp body in his arms and wept.

Look forward to the next installment of the Starfire Ever Moore Series

Made in the USA
Lexington, KY
04 December 2011